Yuanyuan's Bubbles

LIU CIXIN, TRANSLATED BY CARMEN YILING YAN

1

Many people become enraptured by something or other from the moment of their births, as if they came into the world just for the delight of its company. In this way did Yuanyuan become enraptured by soap bubbles.

Yuanyuan was born with an apathetic expression on her face. She even seemed to cry as if she were discharging an obligation. The world was disappointing her greatly, it appeared.

Until, at five months old, she saw soap bubbles for the first time.

Immediately, she began to wave and kick in her mama's lap, her little eyes alight with a radiance that outshone the sun and stars, as if this was the first time she had truly seen the world.

It was noon in the northwest of China, many months since the last rain. Outside the window, the sun-scorched city billowed with dust. In this world of abnormal drought, the gorgeous apparitions of water drifting through the air were truly creatures of utmost beauty. That his little daughter could recognize their beauty gladdened Baba, who'd blown the bubbles for her. Mama, who was holding her, was very happy too. She had waived her remaining month of maternity leave; the next day, she would return to her lab for work.

2

Time passed. Yuanyuan entered the big kid class of preschool, and she still loved bubbles.

This Sunday, she was on an outing with Baba. She had a little bottle of bubble fluid in her pocket: Baba promised he'd have Mama take her up on her airplane to blow bubbles. This wasn't play-pretend;

they really did go to the crude airfield on the city outskirts. The plane Mama used for her aerial seeding research was parked there.

Yuanyuan was quite disappointed. It was a battered agricultural biplane, probably from the Soviet days. Yuanyuan thought it must have been built out of old wood planks, like the hunter's hut in the forest from fairy tales. She doubted it could fly at all. But even so, this shabby plane was off limits to Yuanyuan, according to Mama.

"Today's her birthday!" said Baba. "You're already working overtime here instead of at home with her. At least let her ride on the plane. Give her some fun and excitement!"

"What fun and excitement? She weighs so much already. How many tree seeds will I have to leave on the ground?" Mama said, hauling another heavy plastic sack into the cargo hold.

Yuanyuan didn't think she was all that heavy. She screwed her face up and wailed. Mama hurried over to comfort her daughter, taking a strange object out of one of the big plastic tarp sacks on the ground. It was about the same size and shape as a carrot, pointy-headed and streamlined behind it, with a pair of cardboard tail fins stuck on its butt. It looked like a little airplane bomb, only transparent.

This might be fun. Yuanyuan reached out and touched it, only to immediately draw back: it was made of ice.

Mama pointed to a black speck at the center of the little bomb. She told Yuanyuan that it was a tree seed. "The plane drops these ice bombs from way high up, and when they fall to the ground, they stick into the soil. When spring comes, the ice melts. The water it forms helps the seed sprout and grow. If we drop lots and lots of these ice bombs, the desert will become green, and the sand won't blow into Yuanyuan's face anymore when she plays outside. Mama's research project will double the aerial afforestation survival rate in the Northwest drought areas—"

"What does a kid know about survival rates? Sheesh. Yuanyuan, let's go!" Baba picked Yuanyuan up and marched off. Mama didn't try to keep them, only quickly cupped her daughter's face in her hands one quick last time.

Yuanyuan could feel that Mama's hands were much rougher than Baba's.

From Baba's shoulder, Yuanyuan saw the "hunter's hut" take to the air with a rumble of engines. She blew a string of bubbles toward the plane and watched it disappear into the sandy ether.

Baba carried Yuanyuan out of the airfield to the roadside bus station. As they waited for a bus back into the city, she suddenly felt Baba shiver.

"Baba, are you cold?"

CLARKESWORLD

DECEMBER 2015 - ISSUE 111

FICTION

NON-FICTION

Neil Clarke: Publisher/Editor-in-Chief
Sean Wallace: Editor
Kate Baker: Non-Fiction Editor/Podcast Director
Gardner Dozois: Reprint Editor

Clarkesworld Magazine (ISSN: 1937-7843) • Issue 111 • December 2015

"No . . . Yuanyuan, didn't you hear something just then?"

"Hmm . . . I don't think so."

But Baba had heard it. There had been a low explosion, far off in the direction the plane had been flying, so distant that perhaps he registered it with a sixth sense. He jerked his head around to look back the way they'd come. In front of him and his daughter, the drought lands of the Northwest stared pitilessly toward the vault of heaven above.

3

Time flew onward. Yuanyuan entered elementary school, and she still loved bubbles.

She and Baba visited Mama's grave on Qingming Festival. Like always, she'd brought along her bottle of bubble fluid. As Baba set his flowers in front of the plain tombstone, Yuanyuan blew out a string of bubbles. Baba would have erupted, but her next words left his eyes wet with tears.

"Mama will see them!" Yuanyuan said, pointing at the bubbles floating past the gravestone.

"Child," Baba said as he hugged Yuanyuan, "you have to grow up to be like your mother, with her sense of duty and mission, with a high-minded purpose like hers!"

"I already have a high-minded purpose!" Yuanyuan yelled.

"Tell it to Baba?"

"Blow—" Yuanyuan pointed at her bubbles, already flown far into the distance—"big—*biiiig*—bubbles!"

Baba smiled sadly, shaking his head, and led his daughter away. They weren't far from where the plane had crashed a few years ago. That year, the seeds in the ice bombs dropped from the sky really did survive, growing into saplings, but the final victor had still been the endless drought. The aerially seeded forest had died to the last tree in the dry, rainless second year. Desertification marched inexorably onward.

Baba turned to look back. The setting sun stretched a long shadow behind the gravestone. The bubbles Yuanyuan had blown were all gone now, like the dreams of the woman in the grave, like the beautiful delusion of the Western Development Project.

4

Time flew onward. Yuanyuan entered middle school, and she still loved bubbles.

Today, Yuanyuan's young homeroom teacher had come for a home visit. She handed Baba a flashy, novel-looking toy gun. The physics teacher had confiscated it from Yuanyuan for playing during class, she explained. The gun had a fat barrel and a ring like an antenna loop attached to the muzzle. Baba turned it over in his hands, puzzled as to its appeal.

"It's a bubble gun," said the homeroom teacher, taking it and pulling the trigger. With a low whirr, a long string of soap bubbles shot from the small ring on the muzzle.

The teacher told Baba that Yuanyuan's grades were always the best in her year. Her biggest strength was her robust sense of creativity; the teacher had never seen such a lively-minded student before. He should cherish this seedling, she told him.

"Don't you feel that the child is a bit . . . how do I say this, a bit effervescent?" Baba asked, hefting the bubble gun.

"Hey, all the kids today are like that. Quite honestly, in this new era, being on the light and airy side isn't necessarily a flaw."

Baba sighed, cutting off the conversation with a wave of the bubble gun. He didn't think he and the homeroom teacher had much to say to each other. She was barely more than a child herself.

Once he saw the homeroom teacher off, leaving just the two of them, Baba decided to have a talk with Yuanyuan about the bubble gun. But immediately he encountered a new source of displeasure.

"You bought another one?" he said, pointing to the cell phone hanging from Yuanyuan's neck. "But you already got a new one this year!"

"No I didn't, Baba, I only changed the case! See, it keeps things fresh for me." Yuanyuan took out a flat box as she spoke. Baba opened it, revealing a row of colorful rectangles. At first glance, he thought they were a set of paints. Only upon further examination did he discover that they were twelve cell phone cases in twelve different colors.

Baba shook his head and set the box aside. "I wanted to talk to you about this . . . tendency."

Yuanyuan spotted the bubble gun in his hand and snatched it over. "Baba, I promise I won't bring it to school again!" She shot a string of bubbles at him.

"That's not what I wanted to talk about. The problem goes far deeper than that. Yuanyuan, look, you're a big girl now, and yet you still like to blow soap bubbles—"

"Is that wrong?"

"Oh, no, there's nothing wrong with that in and of itself. It's just that, like I said, your fondness reflects a certain, hmm, mental tendency."

Yuanyuan stared blankly at her father.

"It demonstrates your tendency to chase after pretty, novel, superficial things. You easily lose yourself in mirages. Being so ungrounded in reality will lead you in the wrong direction in life."

Yuanyuan looked at the soap bubbles filling the room, seeming even more puzzled. The bubbles swam tranquilly in the air like a school of transparent goldfish.

"Baba, let's talk about something more interesting!" Yuanyuan leaned against Baba's shoulder and adopted a confidential tone of voice. "Do you think our homeroom teacher is pretty?"

"I didn't notice . . . Yuanyuan, what I was saying was—"

"She's totally gorgeous!"

"I guess . . . I was about to say that—"

"Baba, you have to have noticed the way she looked at you just then, when you were talking. She was really into you!"

"Child, I swear, can't you leave off thinking about these silly things?" Baba irritably peeled his daughter's hand off his shoulder.

Yuanyuan sighed dramatically. "Oh, Baba, you've turned into one of those people who are grumpy about everything. What's the point of living if you never have anything new or interesting or exciting? You should be embarrassed, trying to be a life coach for other people."

A soap bubble drifted in front of Baba's face, then burst. He felt a puff of moist air, almost impossibly faint, and yet the ephemeral little misty drizzle granted him a moment of bliss. It made him think of his distant southern homeland, of all things. He sighed imperceptibly.

"When I was young, I chased after fantasies too. Your mother and I came here from Shanghai, so naive as to think that the Northwest would be a place where we could show the world our worth. In an unimaginably short time, we architects raised an entire, brand-new city out of the wasteland. We thought it would be our life's achievement. After we left this world, this city would stand as proof that we didn't live our lives in vain. Who could have imagined that we'd devoted our best years, and even our very lives, to nothing more than a soap bubble?

Yuanyuan was astonished. "What do you mean, Silk Road City is a soap bubble? It's right here, rock solid. There's no way it's going to vanish with a pop, right?"

"It's about to disappear. The central government has approved the province's report and suspended all new projects to divert water to Silk Road City."

"Do they want us to die of thirst? The taps only work once every two days already, an hour and a half each time!"

5

"They're working out a ten-year evacuation plan right now. The entire city will be dismantled and relocated. Silk Road City will be the first city in today's world to disappear due to water shortages, a modern Loulan . . . In truth, the entire Western Development Project that once had us aflame with passion has already devolved into a nightmarish Western Mining Project. Who knows, that might be an ever bigger soap bubble."

"Wow, that's great!" Yuanyuan cheered. "We should have left this place ages ago! It's so boring here, I really can't stand it! Let's move! Move to a brand new place and start a brand new life! It's going to be amazing, Baba!"

Baba looked at his daughter silently, then stood and walked to the window. He gazed dumbly outside at the city amid yellow sand. His drooping shoulders made his silhouette suddenly appear much older.

"Baba," Yuanyuan called softly, but her father didn't respond.

Two days later, Yuanyuan's father took office as the last mayor of the fading city.

5

Yuanyuan got second place in science on her province's college entry examinations. Baba, truly overjoyed in a way that he rarely was, magnanimously asked his daughter if she had anything she wanted as a reward, even something absurd. Yuanyuan stuck her open hand, fingers spread, in his direction.

"Five . . . five of what?"

"Five bars of Diao brand clear soap." She stuck out her other hand. "Ten bags of Tide laundry powder." She flipped her hands over. "Twenty bottles of White Cat dish detergent." Last, she took out a piece of paper. "Most importantly, I need these chemicals. Buy them in the amounts I listed."

Getting the chemicals took work on her father's part. He had to ask a bureau deputy director going on a business trip to Beijing, who spent a whole day finding them all.

Once she had everything, Yuanyuan holed herself up in the bathroom for three busy days, filling a big washtub with some sort of liquid whose smell permeated into every room in the house. The fourth day, two classmates came over to deliver a custom-made hoop object more than a meter in diameter, shaped from a long piece of metal pipe pricked with small holes.

The fifth day started with a group of visitors. There were two cameramen from different news stations, and the mayor recognized an attractive lady as the hostess of an entertainment program on the provincial channel. There were also two garishly dressed fellows calling themselves adjudicators from the China branch of Guinness World Records, flown in from Shanghai the previous day. One of them said in a hoarse voice, "Mr. Mayor, your daughter—" he broke off, coughing. "The air's awfully dry here. Your daughter is about to set a world record!"

The mayor followed the others onto the apartment building's flat rooftop, where he found his daughter and several of her classmates already there. Yuanyuan was carrying the big hoop. The washtub stood in front of them, filled with the liquid she'd mixed. The two adjudicators went to work erecting two posts with unit markings along their length. Only later did the mayor learn that they were used for measuring the diameter of soap bubbles.

Once the preparations were done, Yuanyuan dipped the hoop into the washtub. When she lifted it out, it was filmed with bubble fluid. She carefully fastened the hoop to the end of a long pole, walked to the building's edge, and waved the pole so that the hoop drew a wide circle in the air, blowing an enormous soap bubble. The bubble shimmered and undulated in midair as if it were dancing. Later, he learned that it was an incredible 4.6 meters in diameter, breaking the Guinness world record of 3.9 meters previously held by Kaj Loos of Belgium.

"The composition of the bubble mixture is important, but the real trick is in this hoop," Yuanyuan said in response to the TV hostess's questions. "The guy from Belgium used an ordinary hoop to blow his bubble, while mine was made by drilling holes along the length of a piece of metal pipe, then bending it into a circle. The pipe is filled with bubble fluid, and as the big bubble forms, the fluid continuously seeps from the little holes, so that as much fluid is available to the bubble as possible. That naturally allows me to blow bigger bubbles."

"Then, do you think you can blow even bigger bubbles in the future?" asked the hostess.

"Of course! It would take research into several important factors in bubble formation, including viscosity, malleability, rate of evaporation, and surface tension. For forming super-big bubbles, the last two need the most work. Rate of evaporation needs to be lowered, since evaporation is the main reason why bubbles burst. As for surface tension . . . do you know why you can't blow bubbles with pure water?"

"Because the surface tension is too small?"

7

"It's actually the opposite. The surface tension of pure water is too high to trap air. For my next question, what's the relationship between a bubble's surface tension and its diameter?"

"Well, from what you've said, the smaller the surface tension, the larger the bubble?"

"Nope! Once the bubble is formed, as the bubble increases in size, it actually needs higher surface tension to maintain its walls. You can see the problem here: the surface tension of a fluid is fixed. In that case, if we want to blow really big bubbles, what problem do we need to solve?"

The hostess shook her head, lost. She was the type hired more for charisma and ease with words than for deeper comprehension. Yuanyuan seemed to realize this. "Never mind, let's blow some more big bubbles for our audience!"

And thus, several more four- and five-meter bubbles drifted in the wind high above the city. In this dry, dust-suffused world, they seemed terribly surreal, like mirages of another world.

One week later, Yuanyuan left the Northwest city of her birth and childhood for the best school of engineering in the country. She was studying nanoscience.

6

Time flew ever onward, but Yuanyuan didn't blow soap bubbles anymore.

Yuanyuan completed her bachelor's degree, master's degree, and doctorate, upon which she built a business with a speed that dizzied her father. Using a technique from her doctorate thesis as a starting point, she invented a new type of solar cell that could be manufactured at a tiny fraction of the cost of traditional monocrystalline silicon cells and adhered in mosaic fashion to completely cover the surface of a building. In just a few years, her business grew to hold assets in the hundred million range, one of the wildly successful entrepreneurships whisked along by the Nanotech East Wind.

Yuanyuan's father thus found himself in an awkward situation. In terms of career success, the daughter was now a higher authority than the father. It looked like Yuanyuan's homeroom teacher from back then was right: being on the light and airy side in thinking and personality wasn't necessarily a flaw. This was an era to make his generation grit their teeth. Success nowadays took overwhelming creative thinking; experience, hard work, a sense of purpose, and so on were no longer decisive factors. Moreover, single-mindedness and solemnity now looked like foolishness.

• • •

"I haven't felt this way in a long time," said the mayor to his daughter, standing on the broad exit terrace in front of the National Center for the Performing Arts. "That was the best performance I've ever heard. The singers really were better than the big three of the olden days."

Yuanyuan knew that opera was one of her father's few pleasures. She'd taken advantage of his business trip to Beijing to invite him to hear a performance by the world's three best tenors of the new generation, given in honor of the impending Olympics.

"I'd have bought the best seats in the house if I'd known. I was afraid you'd call me profligate again, so I just bought two medium-range seats."

"How much did they cost?" Baba asked offhandedly.

"They were much cheaper than before. I think they were 28,000 yuan each."

"Ah . . . wait, what?!"

Seeing her father's wide-eyed, slack-jawed expression, Yuanyuan laughed. "If they made you feel in a way you haven't for a long time, even 28,000 yuan was worth it. Look at this performance center. Why would the government have invested billions in it, if not to help people achieve or recover some kind of emotion through art?"

"Maybe you're right, but I still hope you can spend your money in more meaningful ways. Yuanyuan, I want to talk to you about something related to Silk Road City. Can you invest in one of its municipal projects?"

"What is it?"

"We want to build a large-scale water treatment plant. It'll raise the city's water recycling efficiency by an enormous amount. In addition, it will use solar power to desalinate water from the salt lakes. If this system can be realized, Silk Road City will be able to survive on a reduced scale. It won't have to disappear entirely."

"How much will it cost?"

"By our preliminary plans, about 1.6 billion yuan. We have sources for most of the required funds already, but we can't get our hands on the money for a long time. I'm afraid it might be too late by then. That's why we need you to make an initial investment of about a hundred million."

"Baba, I can't. That's all the liquid assets I have right now, and I wanted to use them for a research project—"

Father raised a hand to break off his daughter's words. "Never mind, then. Yuanyuan, I don't want to hurt your business one bit. To be honest, I hadn't wanted to ask you in the first place. Your investment would break even, guaranteed, but the profit would be miniscule."

"Hah, I wasn't thinking about that, Baba. My project would be even worse. Never mind profit, there's no way it would even earn back the investment!"

"Are you doing theoretical research?"

"No, but it's not practical research, either. I'm doing it for the fun."

" . . . "

"I'm going to develop a super-surfactant. I've come up with the name already, FlySol. Its viscosity and elasticity will be orders of magnitudes better than any liquid existing, and its rate of evaporation will be just a fraction of a percent of glycerin's. And this surfactant will have a special superpower—its surface tension will change depending on the thickness of the liquid layer and the surface's degree of curvature, anywhere between one hundredth and ten thousand times the surface tension of water."

"What is it for?" asked Father in horror. He already knew the answer, but he was afraid to believe it.

The young multi-millionaire put an arm around her father's shoulder. "To blow—big—*biiiig*—bubbles!"

"You're joking, right?"

Yuanyuan looked at the lights of Chang'an Avenue, silent for a long time. "Who knows? Maybe my entire life is a big joke. But, Baba, I don't think there's anything wrong with that. For a person to use their entire life for a joke is a sort of purpose too."

"Spending a hundred million yuan blowing bubbles? Is there any point?" her father spoke as if he were in a dream.

"There's no point. It's fun, that's all. I've got to say, though, compared to the city your generation spent tens of billions building, only to have to tear it down, my extravagance doesn't amount to much."

"But you can save the city right this moment! It's your city too. You were born there. You grew up there. But you're using that money to blow soap bubbles! You're—you're really too selfish!"

"I'm living my own life. Selfless sacrifice isn't always enough to change the path of history. Your own city proves it!"

Father and daughter remained in silence until Yuanyuan steered their car onto Chang'an Avenue.

"I'm sorry, Baba," Yuanyuan said softly.

"These days, I keep remembering the past, leading you by your tiny little hand. It was such a wonderful time." In the light, Father's eyes glimmered, as if damp.

"I know I've disappointed you. You always wanted me to be someone like Mama. If I could live two lifetimes, I'd use one of them to do what you want, give everything for duty and mission. But, Baba, I only have this one life."

Father didn't reply. Near the end of the silent drive, Yuanyuan took out a large envelope and handed it to him.

"What is it?" Father asked, uncomprehending.

"Housing deeds and a key. I bought you a villa by Lake Tai. You'll be able to go back to the south after you retire."

Father gently slid the envelope back in her direction. "No, child, I'm going to live out the rest of my life in what remains of Silk Road City. Your mother and I have buried our youth and dreams there. I can't leave."

Beijing glittered to its heart's content in the summer night. Gazing at the gorgeous sea of lights, Yuanyuan and her father both thought of soap bubbles. What was this boundless radiance trying to show to them: the weight of a life, or the weightlessness?

7

One day, two years later, the mayor received a call in his office from his daughter.

"Happy birthday, Baba!"

"Ha, Yuanyuan, is that you? Where are you?"

"Not far from where you are. I've brought a birthday present!"

"Hey, it's been years since I remembered my birthday. Come home at noon, then. It's been a month since I've gone home myself. There's just the housekeeper there to keep an eye on things."

"No, I'll give you the gift right now!"

"I'm at work. The weekly city council meeting's about to start."

"Not a problem! Open the window and look up!"

The sky today was clear in every direction, a limpid blue, rare weather for the area. The rumble of an engine came from the air; the mayor saw that an airplane was slowly circling in the sky above the city, striking against the blue backdrop.

"Baba, I'm on the plane right now!" Yuanyuan shouted through the phone.

It was an old-fashioned, propeller-driven biplane. In the sky, it looked like a giant bird gliding lazily. Time flashed backward; a familiar sensation struck the mayor like lightning. He shivered all over, as he had done twenty years ago. His daughter had asked him if he was cold.

"Yuanyuan, what—what are you doing?"

"Here's the gift, Baba, pay attention to the bottom of the plane!"

The mayor had noticed earlier that a big hoop hung from the body of the plane. Its diameter was greater than the length of the plane; clearly, it had unfolded into position only after the plane took to the air. Taken together, the plane and the hoop looked like a flying ring. Later, he'd learn that the hoop was constructed like the one Yuanyuan had used to break the Guinness World Record, made of a tube of lightweight metal filled with the nigh-supernatural FlySol. A film of FlySol stretched across the hoop, and innumerable small holes allowed FlySol to continuously flow out of the thin tube that formed the hoop.

An astounding sight appeared. Behind the giant hoop, a bubble was emerging! Refracting sunlight, its form wavered at the edge of visibility. The bubble swelled rapidly; soon, the plane compared to it was only a sesame seed on top of a transparent watermelon.

In the marketplace below, everyone had stopped to look up. People were starting to run out of the city government headquarters building to watch.

The plane circled slowly above the city, tugging the enormous bubble behind it. The bubble had slowed in its growth, but not completely. Gradually, it came to occupy half the sky. At last, it broke loose from the hoop beneath the airplane, floating independently in the air.

"This is my present, Baba!" Yuanyuan shouted excitedly through the phone.

Huge patches of light shimmered in the blue heavens, as if the entire sky were a slick piece of cellophane being crinkled by invisible hands under the sun. On close inspection, the flashes of light delineated an enormous, transparent sphere that took up most of the sky. The people below had to turn their heads nearly one hundred and eighty degrees to see it in its entirety. It looked as if the mirror of heaven were casting a crystalline reflection of the Earth below.

The city began to grow agitated. Traffic jams formed in the thoroughfares.

The enormous bubble slowly descended from the sky. Once it was at a sufficiently low altitude, the people below could even see the city's skyscrapers mirrored on the bubble's surface; as it undulated in the wind, the buildings twisted and distorted, like a kelp forest under the sea. The broad bubble membrane pressed down inexorably. People instinctively shielded their heads with their arms. When the bubble touched the ground, those exposed outside felt a brief itch on their faces as their bodies passed through the membrane.

The bubble hadn't popped. Instead, it had formed a spherical dome nearly ten kilometers in diameter with the ground. The city and the surrounding industrial plants were now trapped in the bubble!

"It wasn't on purpose, it really wasn't!" Yuanyuan said into the camera. "Under normal conditions, the bubble would have floated away in the breeze. Who knew today's wind would be so much weaker than usual? That's why it fell and covered the city!"

The mayor watched the emergency report, which had interrupted the city television station's normal programming. He saw that his daughter was wearing a leather aviation jacket, open at the front to reveal a blue work uniform underneath. Beneath her was the old-fashioned biplane . . . time flashed backward again. *So alike, they look so alike* . . . the mayor's heart melted, tears spilling from his eyes.

Two hours later, the mayor and the newly established emergency team drove to the bubble wall at the city outskirts. Yuanyuan and several of her engineers were there, well ahead of them.

"Baba, isn't my superbubble amazing?" Yuanyuan had lost her earlier panic, her face alight with inappropriate excitement.

The mayor paid no mind to his daughter, raising his head to consider the bubble's surface. The vast sheet of membrane shimmered in rainbow colors under sunlight, intricate patterns of diffraction on its surface shifting and morphing hypnotically in a bewitching sea of all the universe's colors. The membrane was transparent, so that the outside world seen through it was coated with a layer of iridescence too. A certain distance up, the iridescence disappeared; from the air, it would be impossible to see the membrane.

The mayor reached out a hand and carefully touched the superbubble. The back of his hand itched, very faintly: it was already on the other side of the bubble. The membrane might only be a few molecules thick. He drew his hand back through; the membrane instantaneously returned to its original form. The pattern of iridescence there was unchanged, as if it had never been interrupted.

The others also began to touch the membrane, then waved their hands in an attempt to tear it, then at last devolved into flailing punches and kicks . . . but none of it made a difference to the membrane. Every assault passed through the bubble without resistance, after which the membrane restored itself perfectly. With a wave of his hand, the mayor halted everyone's futile efforts. He then pointed to the highway in the distance; the others saw that the traffic on the highway was passing through the membrane undisrupted, even at their high speeds.

"It's like a soap bubble membrane: solid objects can pass through, but not air," said Yuanyuan.

"Air not being able to pass through is the problem. The air quality in the city is rapidly deteriorating," the mayor said, glaring at his daughter.

Everyone looked up and saw that an enormous white dome-shaped cap had appeared in the sky above the city. The membrane was trapping the smoke from the city and industrial plants in the mold of the superbubble. If one were to observe the city from a distance right now, perhaps they'd be seeing a towering hemisphere of milky white.

"We may need to shut down the power plant and the chemical plant to slow down the rate of pollutant release," said the leader of the emergency team. "But the most serious problem is the rising temperatures inside the bubble. Right now, the city is effectively inside a sealed greenhouse without air exchange with the outside world. It's the middle of summer, and the heat from the sun is building up quickly. According to our calculations, the temperature inside the bubble will eventually peak at sixty degrees Celsius!"

"Up to now, what methods have we tried for destroying the super-bubble?" asked the mayor.

"An hour earlier, we had army aviation people fly their helicopters through the top of the bubble, trying to use the propellers to tear it open, but it didn't work," answered an officer from the local garrison. "Then we set explosives where the bubble met the ground. The explosion only made the bubble ripple a while, without causing any damage. Even more incredibly, the membrane instantaneously extended down into the blast crater, traveling right along the bottom without any gap!"

"How long will it take for the bubble to burst naturally?" the mayor asked Yuanyuan.

"Bubble rupture is primarily caused by evaporation of the fluid membrane. This substance has an extremely slow rate of evaporation— even with sunny weather, the bubble will take five or six days to pop," Yuanyuan answered. To her father's outrage, she sounded full of pride.

"Then we'll have to evacuate everyone," the leader of the emergency team said, sighing.

The mayor shook his head. "I won't take that step until we absolutely have to."

"There's another way," said an environmental specialist. "Hurry and have a lot of long tubes made, the wider the better. Place the tubes with one end outside the bubble and a high-power ventilation fan on the other end, and we can exchange air with the outside world."

"Haha—" Yuanyuan started to laugh, startling everyone around her. Surrounded by angry looks, she was laughing so hard she couldn't stand upright. "That idea's—that's hilarious! Haha—"

"This is all your fine work!" the mayor thundered. "You're going to take responsibility and pay back all the losses you've caused the city!"

Yuanyuan looked up at the sky and stopped laughing. "I know, I'll pay up. But I just thought of a simple way to pop the superbubble—burning. Dig a trench one to two hundred meters long where the bubble meets the ground, pour it full of fuel, then light it. The fire will make the membrane evaporate much faster. The bubble should burst after about three hours."

The mayor ordered the emergency team to do as Yuanyuan explained. A wall of fire more than a hundred meters long sprung up on the city outskirts. As the row of furious flames licked at the bottom of the superbubble, strange colors and shapes shimmered in the membrane. The patterns of color revealed that the FlySol from other parts of the bubble was rushing over to replace what had evaporated from the fire, as if the portion being burned had become a giant whirlpool, sucking gorgeous, beguiling floods of color from every direction to disappear into the flames. Their black smoke pressed upward along the bubble's inner surface, gathering into an enormous black hand pressing down, terrifying the millions of city-dwellers within the superbubble.

Three hours later, the bubble popped. People in the city heard a soft tinkle of breaking in the space between heaven and earth, crisp and clear and echoing for a long time after, as if a string in the instrument of the universe had been very gently plucked.

"It's weird, Baba, you didn't blow your top like I thought you would," Yuanyuan said. She and her father stood on the roof of the city government headquarter building, watching the superbubble burst.

"I've been considering something . . . Yuanyuan, I'd like you to answer a few questions for me seriously."

"About the superbubble?"

"Yes. I want to know, since the bubble membrane is impermeable to air from the outside, would the superbubble also be able to retain moist air on the inside?"

"Of course. In fact, toward the end of FlySol's development, I thought of a possible practical application for the superbubbles: giant greenhouses. They could form miniature climate zones in winter, providing temperature and humidity levels suitable for crop growth over large areas. Of course, that would require longer-lasting bubbles."

"The second question: can you make a superbubble float a long way on the wind, for, say, a few thousand kilometers?"

"Not a problem. Heat from the sun accumulates in the bubble, so the air inside expands and creates buoyancy like a hot air balloon's. The superbubble today fell only because it was formed too low in altitude, with too weak of a breeze."

"The third question: can you ensure that the superbubbles burst after a specific length of time?"

"That's doable. We'd only need to adjust the concentration of one of the ingredients to change the solution's rate of evaporation."

"The last question: given enough investment money, can you blow millions, or even billions, of superbubbles?"

Yuanyuan's eyes widened in surprise. "Billions? Heavens, what for?"

"Picture this in your mind: above the faraway sea, countless super-bubbles are forming. Propelled by the strong winds of the stratosphere, they'll set sail on a long journey to ultimately arrive in the sky above northwest China, then burst in unison, scattering the humid ocean air they formed around into our dry air . . . yes, with superbubbles, we can bring in moist air from the seas to the Northwest! In other words, we can bring in rain!"

Shock and emotion left Yuanyuan speechless for a time. She could only look at her father, stunned.

"Yuanyuan, you gave me a glorious birthday present. Who knows, today might prove the birthday of the Northwest too!"

The cool wind of the outside world was blowing over the city. Without the superbubble to confine it, the white dome of smog above was slowly coming apart in the breeze. In the eastern sky, an odd rainbow had appeared. When the superbubble burst, the FlySol in the membrane had scattered into the air to form it.

8

The enormous engineering project to aerially divert water into western China took ten years.

In these ten years, vast sky-nets were built in China's southern waters. The nets were constructed from thin tubes covered in tiny holes. Each eye in the net was hundreds, even thousands, of meters in diameter, similar to the hoop that had blown the superbubble ten years ago, and each net had thousands of such apertures.

There were two types of sky-net: land-mounted and aerial. The land-mounted sky-nets were placed along the coastline, while the aerial sky-nets hung from giant tethered balloons at high altitude, several kilometers above. In the South China Sea and the Bay of Bengal, the sky-nets ran continuously for more than two thousand kilometers along the coast and above the sea, and were nicknamed "The Bubble Wall of China."

The day the aerial water diversion system started up for the first time, the thin tubes in the sky-net filled with FlySol, forming a membrane of fluid over each aperture. Strong, moist sea wind blew into the sky-net, forming countless superbubbles, each kilometers in diameter. The bubbles broke loose from the sky-net one after another, rising in droves to higher skies. Ascending into the atmosphere, they followed the air currents onward, even as more bubbles steadily blew forth from the sky-net. Great flocks of superbubbles glided majestically inland, wrapped around the humid air of the seas. They drifted past the Himalaya Mountains, past the Greater Southwest, into the skies of the Northwest. Between the South China Sea and Bay of Bengal, and northwest China, two rivers of bubbles thousands of kilometers long had formed!

9

Two days after the aerial water diversion system began full-scale operation, Yuanyuan flew from the Bay of Bengal to the capital of a Northwest province. When she stepped off the plane, she saw only a round moon suspended in the night sky: the bubbles that had set out from the ocean had yet to arrive. In the city, crowds were out under the moonlight. Yuanyuan got out of the car at the central square, squeezing her way into the crowd too, to wait fervently along with them.

Even when midnight came, the night sky remained unchanged. The crowd began to disperse as it had the previous two days, but Yuanyuan didn't leave. She knew the bubbles would arrive tonight for certain. She sat on a bench, at the edge of sleep and wakefulness, when she suddenly heard someone cry out.

"Heavens, why are there so many moons?"

Yuanyuan opened her eyes. She really did see a river of moons in the night sky! The countless moons were the reflections in countless massive bubbles. Unlike the real moon, they were all crescents, some curving up and some curving down, all of them so translucent and jewel-like that the real moon seemed plain in comparison. Only by its unchanging location could it be distinguished from the mighty current of moons crossing the sky.

From that point on, the sky over northwest China became the sky of dreams.

During the day, the drifting bubbles were hard to see. There were just the reflections off the membranes, everywhere in the blue sky, that made it look like the surface of a lake rippling under the sunlight. On the ground, enormous but faint shadows traced the slow passage of the bubbles. The most beautiful moments were at dawn and dusk, when the rising or setting sun on the horizon would limn the river of bubbles in the sky with radiant gold.

But these lovely scenes didn't last for long. The bubbles above popped one after another. More bubbles were rolling in, but clouds were beginning to gather in the sky, obscuring the bubbles.

Next, in the season that had been driest of all in previous years, a slow, steady drizzle drifted down from the sky.

Amid the rain, Yuanyuan arrived at the city of her birth. After ten years of evacuation, Silk Road City had become quiet and empty. Unoccupied skyscrapers stood silently in the rain.

Yuanyuan noticed that these structures hadn't truly been abandoned; they were well-preserved, the glass in the windows unbroken. The whole city seemed to be deep in slumber, waiting for the day of revival it knew would come.

The rain tamped down the dust, leaving the air fresh and pleasant. Raindrops tickled deliciously cool on the face. Yuanyuan strolled along streets she knew well, streets through which her father had led her by her small hand countless times, on which countless soap bubbles she'd blown had scattered. A childhood song resounded in Yuanyuan's heart.

Suddenly, she realized that she really could hear the song. The sun had set now, and in the city descended into night, only one window shone with light from within. It belonged to the second floor of an ordinary apartment building, her home, and the song came from there.

Yuanyuan stopped in front of the building. The surroundings were clean and well-kept. There was even a vegetable patch, the plants in it growing heartily. A tool cart stood to one side, fitted with a big metal bucket, clearly used to carry water from elsewhere for the plants. Despite the obscuring darkness, one could sense the breath of life here. In the dead silence of the empty city, it beckoned to Yuanyuan like an oasis in the desert.

Yuanyuan climbed the well-swept stairs and gently pushed open the door to her home. Her father was reclining on the couch, his hair grizzled under the lamplight, contently humming the old children's song. He held the little bottle that Yuanyuan had used to carry bubble liquid as a child, and the little plastic hoop, and he was blowing a string of multicolored bubbles.

Originally published in Chinese in *Science Fiction World*, 2004.

Translated and published in partnership with Storycom.

ABOUT THE AUTHOR

Liu Cixin is a representative of the new generation of Chinese science fiction authors and recognized as a leading voice in Chinese science fiction. He was awarded the China Galaxy Science Fiction Award for eight consecutive years, from 1999 to 2006 and again in 2010. His representative work *The Three-body Problem* won the 2015 Hugo Award for Best Novel, finished 3rd in 2015 Campbell Awards, and was a nominee for the 2015 Nebula Award.

His works have received wide acclaim on account of their powerful atmosphere and brilliant imagination. Liu Cixin's stories successfully combine the exceedingly ephemeral with hard reality, all the while focusing on revealing the essence and aesthetics of science. He has endeavoured to create a distinctly Chinese style of science fiction. Liu Cixin is a member of the China Science Writers' Association and the Shanxi Writers' Association.

Union
TAMSYN MUIR

The wives come strapped ten to a transport, hands stamped by some Customs wonk. Their fingernails are frilled and raised freckles stipple each arm in shades of red and orange. Permit tags list their names: Mary. Moana. Ruth. Myrrh. Huia. Anna. Iridium. Coffee. Kokako.

The Franckton crofters stand and watch from behind the barrier. They've knocked off midday work to come. You can practically see the pong of hot mulch and melting boot elastomeric coming off them. There's even a man there from the *New Awhitu Listener* to take pictures.

Dripping sweat, the Customs detail sign off their quarantine. The wives seem indifferent to the heat. The air from the transport ruffles the thin plaits of their hair, each strand with its own line of fine bulges like a polyp. Everyone is close enough to see.

"If the Listener links any of those photos," Simeon's telling the photographer, "you're dog tucker, mate." Simeon's got the gist of it already. The man knows Simeon's reputation and is timidly pressing *Delete*.

The Mayor signs the receipt of goods slowly. She's asking questions, gesturing at the wives, but she's not getting answers, just filework and shrugging. The Ministry men take the tablet with the signature and you can tell they just want to get the hell out of there before something happens.

Later on when the croft pores over the paperwork, they discover the wives are lichen splices. No one's ever heard of it.

When the news had broken that the Ministry was awarding them wives, the relief was so great in Franckton that it was more pain than pleasure. They'd spent the last fifty years incubating on Governmental loan and mortgaging over half the harvest each time. A lot of beers got sunk during all the frantic budgeting that came subsequently. The staunchest

Union crofters forgot to do anything but tab up how many generations it would take before all they'd be paying for was the foetal scan.

Only Simeon was hostile; nobody was surprised. "It's a disgrace," he kept on saying. "It's a nothing. We're getting gypped. We're the highest-revenue croft and they're shutting us up, they're paying us off, the next time we don't say how high when they say jump we'll get our subsidy slashed and you bastards are falling over yourselves to lick their arse . . . "

He got told off by the Mayor for whinging. The sentiment was that there were only twenty wives to go round and he'd been assigned one and heaps of crofters hadn't. It wasn't as though they were all going to receive rose-splice wives and free beer and skittles. Of course it was a sop. It was a harvest cycle, and the Ministry wanted to keep them sweet so that there wouldn't be a tanty chucked over the price of wheat or onions or oats come the buying time. All of Franckton was going into this with their eyes open; they weren't naive . . . But they still planned a picnic and a pohiri and someone agreed to sing for the welcome and everyone getting a wife washed their shirt.

When the wives finally landed and they got their first eyeful, they knew there wasn't going to be a picnic or a pohiri. They took up their tines and trudged back to the bunds without preamble. Only Simeon, by way of expressing his feelings, threw a big handful of grit at one of the whirring transports. It exploded into a cloud of dusty shrapnel. Some of the crofters cringed, but nothing happened.

The lichen-splice wives are pale and dry. Nobody really knows what to do with them. The last batch of kids had been nine years ago, with a bunch of hardy poppy wives and their minders. They were all hard cases and laughed and made jokes during the incubation, like poppy-wives should. The Mayor was getting treated for germline trouble with her chromosomes 5 and 10, so the Ministry had made them pay through the nose for gene insurance and they'd all been sore about it, but not too sore because it was the Mayor and the croft begrudged her nothing. Simeon had squabbled and said there should be a lawsuit. Some of the crofters agreed, but then there were children to take care of and nobody did anything.

The first thing the crofters hate is the names. Their wives have been given croft names, and that's insult to injury, somehow. It's ingratiating. They should have had city names and all been Florence or Hannah or Candy. So they all become "wife" by common fiat.

They seem obliging enough, but they never speak, except sometimes "Yes" or "No." They move slowly in the Franckton heat, but unmindingly.

They are slow in general to walk or to carry. They lid their eyes heavily when they talk and keep their mouths a little open, sometimes flickering their tongues.

Simeon holds forth in the pub almost every night about them. Most of the croft complaints are about how their wife stares or can't cook the tea right or is stupid, or off-putting, or intractable, but Simeon goes further than that. "I don't want to incubate with some knock-off government sack," he says of his wife. "She looks like a spastic. She looks like a trisomy hutch."

Some of the croft look away but they don't protest, because you don't with Simeon, it's more trouble than it's worth. Simeon says, "I bloody well mean it. And I tell you what, if they don't bear good kids and look after them right, I'm blowing this wide open. I'll strike. I want our next lot to have a future, not go on cringing like mutts for crusts. If all the crofts got up off their bums and stood together we'd have the world on a plate. Look at what we get when we don't fight for it! Christ, look."

Outside the pub and across the street two of the wives stand in the blue evening shade. Simeon stabs a finger in their direction. They do not chat or relax: they stare, first at each other, then at a crack in the daub house, then at a drying clag of mulch, then at each other again. Their tongues flicker in their mouths.

"I tell you what," Simeon says again, "they scare me to death. They're not right. We got fobbed off with something weird, and we're just shutting up and taking it like we always do."

One of the crofters has the bright idea to tell Simeon that he should have let the photographs go live, that everyone should have seen what had been done to Franckton. This crofter gets pranged with the beer mat.

"Don't be stupid," snaps Simeon, settling back. "We've got our bloody pride."

Franckton has better results with the wives in the fields. The sun leaves white patches on their skin if they stay out too long in it, but the Mayor gets the children to weave them big scratchy shapeless hats. The wives have been taught to say, "Thank you, Aunty," and for each hat a wife intones "Thank you, Aunty," before subsiding back into silence. They're still slow out there on the bunds, but they are just as slow heaving the stones between them as they are walking as they are everything else. It is simply how they move. They crouch down and poke back rocks into the spillways with their square, dry hands. They build back the gullies and do not care. When the children come around with the water they take one gourd together and sip miniature sips, darting their tongues inside the neck of the bottle. The other crofters take enormous gulps and dump the rest down the backs of their hot, dirty necks.

It gets to some of the croft. Nobody dares to be as bad as Simeon, who calls his wife "you" and who swaps sharp words with the Mayor about it almost daily, but there's loads of complaint. The wives don't learn. They don't settle. They're lazy. They make everyone uneasy. Plenty of splice wives are good for doing chores and croft work—so the catalogues always promise—and do it cheerfully and well, but these ones don't, and it's yet another black eye for them.

When Laura says in the pub, "I like my wife," everyone's surprised into silence before they bust a gut laughing. "Piss off! I don't mind her. I wouldn't want one that was talking my ear off all the time. And she sings sometimes . . . She's not so bad."

She gets ragged for this daily, but sticks to it: "Mary's a good girl," she goes on saying staunchly. "She gives it heaps, just doesn't rush. Can't believe you're all moaning about how they don't have tea on the table when the clock strikes six. My God! You lot don't know you're born."

Those with wives start noticing that, wherever they go, a fine leafy build-up appears on the walls or countertops where they work. This is easily wiped off with a damp cloth, but causes no end of alarm. The build-up is a thin crust—a substrate with miniature flakes—dusty green in some houses, shrillingly orange in others. Simeon spits the dummy entirely and makes his wife sleep in the shed, and at this point nobody blames him, he's sent a sample to the big lab in Awhitu and it matches the wives' DNA. Like they're shedding, the pharmacist had said helpfully. "Like they're moldy," said Simeon. "Bloody hell. It's not clean. It's filthy. It's not right. They oughtn't to, it's a decay, they're off-cut bargain-bin splices—" And he calls them a lot worse than *off-cuts* or *bargain bin splices*.

He sends a letter to the Ministry representative, a formal one, with a couple veiled threats chucked in. Other crofters are angry too, and they sign it. The Mayor won't.

"It's harmless," she says wearily, "it's a nothing. Just rub a bit of ti-tree extract on the counter, the pharmacy let me have it for cheap. And if you're making Coffee sleep in the shed you better not whinge about her cooking."

But Simeon won't let his wife do any cooking now. She shouldn't touch food, he says. Shouldn't touch anything they're not sure about. As per usual, some of the croft privately agrees, but also wishes he'd stop being a bit of a tosser.

The doctor comes to give the crofters their health certificates and the Mayor her latest injections. They can't apply for the DNA license otherwise. He frowns over the Mayor's scans—again—and gives her some chromosome duplicant on the sly, in exchange for a feed and some cash. "I'm sorry, Barbs," he says. "You'll be paying the premium again for the license."

"But I'm not contributing," she says, surprised. "Not after the last time. Didn't we put that down on the form?"

"Doesn't matter; still shows up on your insurance record, I'm afraid. It's a generational issue. It's not just your license, it's all of Franckton's."

"That is daylight robbery," says the Mayor, "not a deterrent."

"It's a damned shame is what it is," says the doctor, "but there's nothing you or I could've done about it. At least you're not renting the cow to get the milk this time, eh?"

It's true. They're not coughing up for wife costs. Simeon still writes savage letters to the croft's Parliamentary manager but now they're getting answered by auto-message. They've got to take out a loan against the harvest, which stings, and nobody lets the Mayor put her personal savings in to help, but there's softer words about the wives when the croft thinks about all the money they're saving. Fewer people laugh at Laura. There's enough to pay for a couple of multiples in kids. The last generation born of the whānau is old enough to babysit, but now there's the wives to do the care, so they can stay at school instead. Not one crofter has got to stay at school past the age of twelve before. An out-of-towner can't visit Franckton now without getting buttonholed and skited to for half an hour about their good fortune. They book the extraction and the foetal care unit for Christmas.

The weather gets hotter and hotter. The wives are in trouble.

A pruinose bloom settles on the northern oats bund. A feathery patina is discovered on the uppermost parts of the stalk—none on the roots—and it can be wiped off in much the same way as the house crust. The wives stand around dispassionately, hands stuck in their aprons, just watching. The croft explodes in tight-lipped fury. They call a meeting at the public house before the heat of the morning's even in ripeness and everyone's there but the children and wives.

"Here is what we know," says the Mayor. "The growth isn't parasitic. The crop isn't spoiling—yet. We've probably caught this in time. We'll take the girls off bund duty and go on from there."

"That's not what *I* know," says Simeon.

He slams his mattock down on the table, in full flight. "Here's what *I* know," he says. "I know that we paid *twenty thousand* for seed DNA that wouldn't get heat rot or spore. I know that we've been bled dry in licenses and mito checkers and quarantines and chromosome therapies, and that's been long as I live, and I know that we're bloody indentured slaves—" ("Too right," says somebody) "—and that these wives, they looked nice on paper but they're sabotage, they're Ministry sabotage, trying to keep us down. Stop the crofts growing out of control. We've mortgaged those bloody oats and if they bloody spoil then we're dead bloody meat."

He says this very fast. The Mayor says, "Simeon—"

"We should ship them back now and to hell with the incubation, show them we don't take hand-outs, eh," he says, voice rising. "We don't take hand-outs! We don't take pay-offs, we don't get tricked!"

A brief pause chills the air. "You're paranoid, mate," says Laura, and a mad hubbub breaks out.

There's lots of noise. The crofters all shout to be heard. If Parliament wants the croft to stay small, why give them incubation rights? Well, it's a con, isn't it. Remember the story about the old horse. The gift horse, the Greeks. Why would the other crofts stand with them? The other crofts look out for themselves. Simeon's going to get everyone arrested. Laura's got her head in the sand. Simeon's right. Everyone's a coward. They should send back the wives. They shouldn't send back the wives. They should have sent back the wives long ago. "If those oats fail I'll send them back in a box," bellows Simeon.

The Mayor whacks one big, hard hand down on the table. Everything on it rattles percussively.

"Shut up!" she roars. "Shut up, all of you!"

"You act like serfs, you get treated like serfs!" Simeon's still ranting. "You all go along with it, you all *let it happen!*"

The Mayor yanks off her shoe, and she throws it square at Simeon. It clips him lightly on the shoulder. He turns very red. The quiet that ensues is greasy and awful. The breath of each crofter comes slight and small, so as not to make too much of a noise.

"I won't have such talk," says the Mayor slowly. "You besmirch us. You take away from the whole croft. You do us damage."

The silence squirms like a child. The croft becomes aware that the wives have gathered in the doorway. They stand there with dull, slabby faces and their floppy hats in their hands. Only their tongues seem awake, spasmodically flicking behind their teeth, pattering against the inside of each cheek.

One of the wives says, "We're sorry, Aunty," and the rest follow in a monotone chant, "We're sorry, Aunty," all slightly out of time. Simeon's wife says it last.

"I'm bloody out," says Simeon, and he shoulders past them, stumbling. The door of the public house rattles on the doorframe when he slams it.

"Do you know what you're sorry for?" says the Mayor, addressing the wives now. The wives do not speak. Some of them look at her, or out of the window, or at the floor, or at a fixed point nowhere in particular. Not a one blinks. The wheezing air conditioner ruffles the thin whippy polyps of their braids. The Mayor repeats, sternly: "There's no use in being sorry for no reason. Wives are meant to help, not to cause trouble. There's mold all over the oats. Do you know how to stop it?"

There is a long silence. One of the wives ventures, "It is very dry," and the other wives pick up on this non-sequitur eagerly, blandly repeating: "It is very dry," and one wife, Laura's, says: "Getting drier."

An impatient sigh rises from the crowd.

"Stay out of the fields," says the Mayor. "You can go out and take over the goats from the children. They can spend their afternoon in the classroom instead. No going near the crops. Is that clear?"

By the blank expressions, it is not. But when the Mayor repeats, "Stay out the fields for now. Understand?" it's greeted with a chorus of *yes, Aunty*. Then they file out of the building and stand around in the shade in an awkward gaggle. Some of them stare through the window. The crofters think it's no use.

The wives are right about one thing: it's dry and getting drier, and the dry season hasn't even started. There's no rainfall and no sign of one to come. The water levels in the Franckton tanks dip lower and lower.

It takes a few days, but the croft manages to wipe the crust off the oat spikelets without too much difficulty. Some of it succumbs, gets blotchy or the stem thickens and blights beyond repair—and the lack of rain's not helping—but after a few days of holding their breaths they start to exhale. No further bloom forms. The kids all have a moan about extra school.

The wives drift around and keep watch over Franckton's goats. There are only so many goats, and really most of the goats spend their time hiding in the goat ark away from the sun. The wives cluster in the shade and listlessly fold laundry, or don't pretend to do anything at all but stare at the dust and the sky and the goat ark. They are unperturbed by the stifling heat and the grit whipping up everyone else's sleeves.

They'll harvest the standing grain the moment it's ready. There's no worry that it won't be dry. The onions will come later. It's another cost to get the silos and augers cleaned and tested, but when the results come in clean the croft wipes the sweat off their brow and gets the grain in. Everyone's busy driving the trucks over from the depot, or checking up on the old harvester, talking about the price of phosphines, and nobody has time to worry about the goats or the wives.

Nobody even notices the goat's sick. It just keels over one day. They find it with three of the wives clustered around, three matching expressions of pallid bemusement.

There is a fine crumbly crust all over the dead goat's head. Wispy filaments are clustered thickly around its ears and damp, flared nostrils, protruding in bunches that deform the skin from beneath. Tiny sprigs sprout from each cornea of the bubbly blind eyes. The mouth's full. Most of the growths are around the skull, though there are raised, crinkly plates of lichen painting the moist belly and anus.

All the croft gets out of the bunds without even scraping their boots. The only ones not in the public house are the vet and the vet assistant, checking and testing the rest of the stock. Everyone sits around, hats squeezed tight between their knees, hands quietly wrung together.

"I'll do it," says Simeon haggardly.

None of the croft answer. He says, "First crop, now stock. We've lost thousands if that herd's gone. I always said we paid too much to get them in utero, but they're good uncloned milch goats." Everyone remains silent. "And it's not just money. There's us to think about as well—us and the young ones."

When nobody says a word, not a word, he shouts: "You bastards. Pull finger already. Don't make me make all the decisions when you're just as scared as I am."

The Mayor sets down the grainy photos of the dead goat and says, "Don't tell us what we already know, Simeon. Make a proposal."

"Single shot to the back of the head," says Simeon.

Laura rises with red clutched fists, spluttering, but the crofters around her yank her down into her seat. The Mayor says, "We could send them back—"

"How long will that take? It's days and days for the ambo to get through. They needed to be out of here yesterday. "

Someone else suggests turning them loose, taking them out of the boundary and into the dusts, and the Mayor says shortly, "I wouldn't turn a dog loose into that," and Simeon says, "What if they got to another croft, for Chrissakes? Don't pass the buck. It's our problem. It's not our fault but it's our bloody problem."

Laura barks, "You can't be serious."

"Deadly. You come up with a better plan, then. Go on." When another crofter says that they'll get arrested for this, they'll get the officers in, Simeon laughs mirthlessly. "That's what you're bleating about? The plod getting us for property damage? The Ministry signed them over to us. If it's the inquest you're worried about, by God, just let me take the rap. I've been wanting my day in court for years. None of the rest of you will get blood on your hands, I'll put them down. I'm not watching our stock die and our kids get sick and us bled dry for doctor bills—God, I could kill them all!" he ejaculates. "It's what they wanted all along, they sent us toxic waste!"

He takes off his hat and he scrunches it between his hands. "I'll do it," he says. "And I'll cop it when the Ministry comes."

The Mayor says in a voice like grit, "I will call a vote. A show of hands, please, for those in favor."

A couple of hands shoot up, immediate and grim. Simeon's nodding. Others rise more slowly. The clock ticks the minutes. The final few are unwilling, like a held breath let out. The Mayor's hand is among these stragglers. Laura's the only one who doesn't have her hand up in all the croft, and nobody meets her eye.

She's crying out: "You arsehole, Simeon. You always hated them, admit it." But Simeon's already putting his hat on his head and heading out the door. Nobody rises to go with him. Nobody shifts from their seat.

They can see it from the window: the wives gathering up behind Simeon when he beckons, collecting them from the shady decks and from the field. They all troop together down the street, the wives placid, their tongues flickering in their mouths, some of them looking through the window back at the silent crofters with their thin eyelids half-down over their dusty eyes. Simeon disappears into his shed and reappears with his shotgun and the wives bob after him, one by one, down to the old abattoir.

At the first crack of gunshot the Mayor sits down at the table and covers her eyes, and she makes a low, guttural sound in the back of her throat. They count one, two, three. A flinching pause between each. At the twentieth it stops. Everyone waits for no reason at all in the silence that follows, a fidgeting, shuffling, throat-clearing quiet.

When she can apparently bear it no longer, the Mayor snaps, "You all go get your tools and dig a pit past the boundary. Tell the vet to burn the goat." One of the croft asks about the kids. "Say to the children we sent them away. Enough of this, already!"

• • •

They wrap the wives in bits of old sacking and put them in a shallow pit past the croft boundary, and they cover them up in sand and gravel and spray the bed with fluorescent paint to mark where they're laid. They burn the goat and keep the others under watch. They work until past the time when the light has all gone, fixing the bunds, taking the temperature in the silo, steaming the winnower in preparation to take it back to the depot. Those who had wives go home to empty houses and Laura doesn't go at all, just cracks open tinnies in the public house and curses anyone who comes near her. Simeon doesn't go home either but hoses out the abattoir.

"Thank God that's over," he repeats, cold and bluff, to anyone on the street he can collar, which isn't many. "Bring on Christmas. That's what I say." He sits on his deck and cleans his gun by sickly solar light, and every so often says "Bring it on," quietly, still somehow audible through closed croft doors and shuttered croft windows, the croft lying awake in their beds.

The onion harvest demands all Franckton's attention. The weather station promises a lot of rain in a month's time and that means hurry, to hoe down the stalks and get the crop ready for dry-curing. After that will be soil prep and nitrogen checkers and sifting and seed negotiation and prices. There's too much to do. There's twenty fewer pairs of hands to do it with. Christmas bears down on them, inevitable and hot, like a sunburn.

The rain starts off Friday as a percussive clap of thunder. The clouds gather in fat, hot, bluish puffs above the croft, and then they open up and the rain roars out. The onions get hauled off in haste to the gas room. The kids are chivvied, screaming, off to the fields to pick up abandoned clippers and pins, jandals slapping noisily on the macadam. The racks groan under the weight of stacked vegetables, frantically checked over for lichen must. One rack shows neck rot but that's par for the course, to be honest, no matter how much they pay for fungal-resistant seed strains or official pesticides it's never a done deal. Simeon says it just goes to show they had a near miss and everyone pretends they haven't heard him.

The whole croft's stuck inside, gloomily playing at cards or smoking. Friday, Saturday, Sunday, Monday, the rain comes down. The sealed road is steamy, liquidy. The warehouse is a blast furnace of dry onion air. The kids all cavil at the rain and the goats get put in the big shed when the ark proves to have a leak. The spraypainted place where the wives were bundled blurs into a watermark.

The thunder comes back and rolls around the plain up and down, booming and growling, startling everyone just when they think it's gone away. There's a lot of joyless boozing in the public house. Nobody has anything to talk about after they've used up the topics of the harvest, the rain. All the water sinks into the dust.

A few days before Christmas the croft wakes up and their wives are back. All over Franckton, the watery sunrise limns wives cooking breakfast, wives sitting patiently in chairs, wives making mash for the goats, wives standing in the corners with their tongues flickering in their mouths and their eyes looking nowhere. Laura doesn't even notice her wife in her kitchen or the egg-frying smells until the plate is put in front of her on the table, and then she screams out loud.

The goats butt from behind the door in the big shed, bawling to be let out. The wives seem distantly astonished by all the fuss: crofters slamming open the peeling dust-screen doors, shouting, hauling on daggy bedrobes and slippers. Inside, Laura reaches out with a jittering hand to push aside the muddy polyppy strands behind her wife's ear: sees the healing weal, powdery, an angry-looking half-closed hole, the dull sheen of a bullet inside the skull being slowly pushed out. Her wife jerks her head away a little, like she's ticklish. Other than the weal she is a nice yellow-green color all over, her freckles a brilliant carmine, her nails as rippled as a riverbed.

The Mayor is panting down the street in her pajamas, an old mackintosh wrapped around her shoulders. She is calling for help.

In Simeon's house, the door has been wrenched from its hinges. There is a fearful amount of broken crockery in the sink. Chairs have been pushed over. Next to the kitchen table lies Simeon, legs and arms akimbo. They can only tell it's Simeon by the clothes, because his skull is a stoved-in mash, fuzzy with the must, sprouting and foliose at the mouth and eye-sockets. Spongy lobes of plant matter rim out down his neck. Gouts of bloody lichen have detonated out his chest, nestled down between brackets of white cracked rib. Long fronds radiate outwards from holes at the stomach: wet with blood, wet with matter, spiraling upwards, drying. He seems titanic in death, enormous and monstrous, half-person, half-explosion.

There are footprints everywhere in the dust, heaps of them. When they go to check on the shed out back there's Simeon's wife, sitting peacefully on her cot. She stares implacably past them, only occasionally reaching up to fret at the hole behind her ear. She yawns with a wet mouth and bright green teeth. When they ask her questions, she gives them a vague smile.

Laura finishes retching behind the goat ark and rejoins the croft, meeting for what feels like the umpteenth time in the pub. All the croft looks old all of a sudden. The Mayor's mackintosh hangs off one shoulder as she sits in a groaning chair.

"Well," she says, and seems unable to say anything but, "Well."

"Well, what?" demands Laura. "What the hell are we going to tell the Ministry?"

The whole croft mulls this one over. They'll have to register Simeon's death. There ought to be someone who comes for the remains, but most of the time nobody does, that's a fact. One of the crofters says that anyway it's three days until Christmas, and nobody will come out to them before the new Ministry calendar year. And someone else says what about the extraction and care team.

"That's not what I bloody meant," says Laura, "what do we *do*?"

Franckton's already paid for the foetal care team and all the licensing. They won't notice the damage to the wives, will they? Probably not. They only look munted if you get up close, check them out carefully. Nothing a bath won't fix, either. They've paid for everything. There's the harvest to think about. The Ministry's more trouble than it's worth to talk to. This whole thing's been a muck-up from start to finish.

"They've *killed Simeon*," says Laura.

The Mayor has an expression like rock ice. She meets Laura's terrified eyes, and Laura sees the fear reflected in hers, the fishlike darting of the pupil. There's a shuffling outside. A lot of the wives have gathered by the door. The whole croft turns to look at them: twenty dull, dispassionate expressions, mud streaks on flexing fingers. Some of the wives have put on new aprons, but the ones who haven't have big blooming brownish stains on each breadth. They look expectant. They look supremely calm. They look healthy and green and moist.

One of them is at the door and they didn't even see her move.

"Do we look after the goats, Aunty?"

The Mayor stares at her—stares right through her. After a moment she says, "No. There's clearing up today, after the rain. Tell—tell the other girls to go home."

"Yes, Aunty," she says, and she's gone with the rest.

There's silence in the pub. An empty, wavering silence, like a heat shimmer. Anticipatory. Laura says faintly, "We need to tell someone . . ."

"We've got our bloody pride," says the Mayor.

The crofters are all picking up their slippers and their mugs and are smoothing back their hair, drifting homewards to re-start the morning. Numbly, Laura does the same, retracing her steps, sliding open the mossie screen on her front door. The eggs on her breakfast plate are cold. Her wife is back and running plates under the dry-cleaner, laboriously picking off bits of dried food, singing tunelessly. Laura notices the bloody splotches on the hem of her dress.

"Welcome home," says her wife.

Sweat beads at the middles of Laura's palms.

The rest of the croft settles down and plans the pohiri they'll have to welcome the conception-care team, and a picnic. The Ministry announces that they'll be given five percent off foetal mitochondrial therapy, on account of it being Christmas. Everyone contributing to a baby washes their shirt.

ABOUT THE AUTHOR

Tamsyn Muir is a writer from Auckland, New Zealand, currently teaching in the United Kingdom. Her short-form horror fiction has appeared in such publications as *Nightmare Magazine, Weird Tales,* and *The Magazine of Fantasy & Science Fiction.*

Morrigan in Shadow
SETH DICKINSON

capella 1/8

She's falling into the singularity.

Straight off her nose, shrouded in the warp of its mass, is the black hole that ate a hundred million colonists and the hope of all mankind.

So Laporte throttles up. Her fighter rattles with the fury of its final burn.

Spaceflight is about orbits. That's how one thing relates to another, up here: I whirl around you. I try to pull away. You try to pull me in. If we don't smash each other apart, or skip away into the void, maybe we can negotiate something stable.

But Laporte has learned that sometimes you just need to fall.

Her instruments don't understand what's happening. They're military avionics, built to hunt and kill other warships (other people) in cold flat space. Thus Laporte flies her final mission in a screaming constellation of errors, cautions, icy out-of-range warnings. An array of winter-colored protests from a machine that doesn't know where it is or why it's about to die.

She wants to pat the ship (a lovely, lethal, hard-worn Uriel gunship, built under Martian skies, the skies of her lover's childhood) on its nose and say: there, there, I know exactly how you feel. I'm with you, man. This shit is beyond me.

But it's not beyond her. She knows why she's here.

Laporte never thought she'd be a good soldier. Certainly she'd never planned to be an exceptional killer. Or a mutineer leading a revanchist fleet up out of Earth's surrender and into a crusade across the length of human space. Or, in her final act as a human being (if she dares make claim to that title any more), the avatar of an omnicidal alien power with no intelligence, no awareness, and a billion-year-old cosmic imperative to destroy all higher thought.

But she is all those things now. Born from the tragedy of a war as unnecessary as it was inevitable. Shaped by combat and command and (between it all, pulling in the opposite direction) the love of the finest woman she's ever met.

After all that, after Simms and NAGARI and That Revelation Ken, she knows why she's here. She knows what force plucked her out of paradise and fired her down the trajectory of her short, violent life. To this distant terminus where the universe folds up behind her into a ring of light, everything she loves, everyone she's hurt, receding.

She knows what she's come to kill. The object of her last assassination.

"Boss, this is Morrigan," she tells her flight recorder. "I am descending towards the target."

That's what she calls Simms, even now. Not 'love'. Boss.

There are three stories here, although they are all one:

What happened in Capella, at the end.

What happened with NAGARI, at the beginning.

What happened between Noemi Laporte and Lorna Simms, which is the most important story, and the one that binds the others.

It begins with the war, and with Lorna Simms—

simms 1/9

For a long time, long enough to murder tens of thousands of people, Laporte thought Simms was dead.

They fought for the United Earth Federation in the war against the colonist Alliance. Laporte and Simms were Federation combat pilots (SQUADRON VFX-01 2FM/FG2101 INDUS—The Wargods, Captain Lorna Simms Commanding) and they were good, so good, they fought like two fists on a drunken boxer, moved by instinct and kill-joy. Of course, a boxer has a body as well as a pair of fists—but they tried not to consider the shape of what connected them.

It wasn't love or lust alone (they were soldiers and their discipline held), nor was it only respect, or fear, or sly admiration. Something of all of this. Whatever connected them, it helped them fight. Simms the Captain, leader of killers, and Laporte her faithful wingman, who was the finest killer.

And they fought to save their Federation, their happy humanist utopia, Earth and Mars and the Jupiter moons—a community of people making each other better. They fought hard.

The war is a civil war. As intimate and violent and hard to name as the bond between Laporte and Simms. An apocalyptic exchange of fratricides between the Federation and its own far-flung interstellar colonists: the Alliance.

For a little while, long enough to give them hope, Laporte and Simms and their Wargods almost won the war.

Then the Alliance clockmaker-admiral, the cryogenic bastard Steele, set a trap. It caught Simms, Laporte, and their whole squadron. Everyone died. It was like a lesson: no band of heroes will save you. No soldiers bound by law and decency.

Out of that ambush Simms and Laporte flew each other to refuge, but it was not refuge enough, the war was in their bones and flesh now: Simms was dying, poisoned by radiation. So they sat together on a crippled warship and they talked about anything but each other.

Remember that? After the ambush at Saturn? Remember adjusting Simms' blankets and pressing your cheek to her throat? Hoping she'd live long enough for both of you to die together, as you'd always dreamed?

(Laporte's dreams are not, it turns out, wholly her own.)

The Alliance was winning, they agreed. Neither of them could see a way to avoid defeat. Neither of them would admit that to the other—not defeat, nor the other thing between them.

Simms passed out. Laporte stayed by her side.

And then a rescue ship came, and with it came al-Alimah, the woman with the gunmetal eyes and the shark-sleek uniform of a Federation black ops officer. She came to tempt Laporte away from Simms with the promise of her other love—

Victory. Al-Alimah came to offer Laporte a chance at victory. And she named the agents of that victory NAGARI.

nagari 1/10

What is victory? Only a fool goes to war without an answer.

The Alliance is winning (has won). What is their victory condition? Their grievance? The fatal casus belli that sparked it all?

The Federation is a gentle state, built on Ubuntu, a philosophy of human connection. So they say: the war began because the Alliance couldn't stand to be alone. They spent two decades rebuilding the severed wormhole to Earth, so they could demand reunification, so they could mobilize our thriving economy to build their warships. So they could galvanize our culture for war.

What the Alliance asked the Federation is what the woman named al-Alimah asked Laporte, as they stood together over the radiation-cooked body of Lorna Simms: give up your gentle ties. Come with me, towards victory. Become a necessary monster.

When the Federation refused to militarize, the Alliance invaded. It was their only hope.

Either they gained the Federation's riches, or they faced the Nemesis alone.

Laporte, she made the other choice, the one her beautiful home could not. She went with al-Alimah. She joined the phantom atrocity-makers called NAGARI and she discovered her own final hope, her endgame for Federation victory.

It'll require the extermination of the entire Alliance population. So be it. She is an exceptional killer. She proved that after she left Simms.

That's how she ended up here, at this raging dead star on the edge of Alliance space, this monument to the power of the alien Nemesis. The tomb of Capella—

capella 2/8

Back in the now: and someone's chasing her.

She sniffs him out by the light of his engines. Something's come through the wormhole behind her and started its own plunge towards the (terrible, empty, fire-crowned) black hole.

Laporte grins and knocks her helmet twice against her ejection seat, crash crash, polymer applause for the mad gentleman on her trail. She knows who it is. She's glad he's come.

She tumbles the Uriel end-for-end so that she's falling ass-first into oblivion and her nose is aimed back, up, towards the universe. There's a ring of night and bent starlight all around her, where the black hole's gravity bends space, but up above, as if at the top of a well, are the receding stars.

And there he is. A fierce blue light which resolves into the molybdenum greatsword-shape of an Alliance strike carrier. *Atreus*. Steele's flagship. Two and a half kilometers of tactical divinity.

Admiral Onyekachi Tuwile Steele prosecuted the war in the Sol theater. A game of remorseless speed chess with fifteen billion pawns in play. In the end, after the Federation exhausted all its gambits and defenses (save one, the one called NAGARI), he won the war.

He's a perfectionist, Steele. A man of etiquette and fine dress, a man who moves like a viper or a Kinshasa runway model. He makes intricate, clockwork plans, predicated on perfect understanding of his opponent's behavior. He cannot abide error.

He made only one.

Nowhere in the final hours of the war, the Mars gambit, the desperate defense and ultimate failure of SHAMBHALA, did he send enough hunter-killers to eradicate Laporte.

And now he has come a-howling after her, propelled by portents and terrors, operating on a desperate, improvised logic. That logic might be: if she wants it, I cannot permit it. If Laporte reaches for a thing, I must deny it to her. She is too dangerous to ever have a victory.

It might be something else. It's dangerous to let your enemy understand your war logic.

simms 2/9

There are three stories here. They all matter.

One is the story of Laporte at Capella, trying to kill billions. That's the ending.

One is the story of Laporte leaving Simms for NAGARI, in the name of victory. That's the beginning.

But in between them is another story, because the road from victory to genocide passes through love. In this middle part, the Federation's civilian government surrendered to the Alliance. And here in the ashes Laporte found Simms alive, Simms found Laporte still (barely) human, they each found the other in the cold scorched wolfpack of the Federation Navy, lurking on the edge of the solar system and contemplating mutiny.

This story is the most important, because it was Laporte's last chance to be a person again.

So: Laporte reaches for Simms. She wants to be close again. She wants to come back.

They're lying side by side in the avionics bay of Laporte's fighter: an alloy coffin as cold as treason. Mostly empty. The terms of the cease-fire have stripped all military electronics from the Federation Navy.

Like their uniforms—taken too. They work in gym clothes and mechanic's overalls. Whenever they breathe the vapor spills out white like a suitbreach. Every ten minutes a dehumidifier clicks on.

Simms shivers. Her hands rattle and she breaks the test pin she's using against the teeth of a server stack. "Shit," she says, closing her eyes. "Fuck."

She survived radiation poisoning. But surviving a wound doesn't erase it. You only rebuild yourself around the scar.

Laporte knifes the RESET switch up, down, up, down. They'll start over. "Slowing me down, boss," she says, trying to take Simms' fear and judo it around, make it funny, disarm its violence. "Slowing me down."

"Fuck you too." Simms clenches and unclenches her fists, one finger at a time. She's longer than Laporte, and stronger. Before she soaked up fifteen grays of ionizing radiation, she could always keep up. "*You* try fingerbanging a combat spacecraft after a lethal dose."

Laporte makes a wah-wah baby noise. Simms laughs. They work for a few more minutes and soon they've made the fighter ready to hold combat software in the spare memory of its navigational systems.

If they're going to mutiny, the mutiny needs its fighters. And Laporte is planning a mutiny.

Simms puts down the test pin and shivers from her scalp to her toes. She looks silver-gold, arid. She is the child of Mongolian steppe and American range and the desert of Mars. She's used to cold. Laporte's afraid that it's not the cold making her shiver. Simms has been listening, the last few days, as Laporte lifts up her scabs and talks about NAGARI, and about her plan for victory.

"They took out all my bone marrow," Simms says. "I'm full of fake bone shit. Medical goo."

Laporte rolls into her (the old words, in a pilot's brevity code: *Boss, Morrigan, tally, visual, press,* It's you, I'm me, I see you, I will protect you) and Simms puts an arm around her. Laporte kisses her under the jaw, very softly, and rests her ear against Simms' collarbone. There's a plastic button rubbing into her cheek but she doesn't mind.

"Seems to work okay," she says. She looked up radiation therapies: desperate transplant of reprogrammed skin cells and collagen glue. She imagined them peeling the skin off Simms' thighs to fill up her bones.

"Yeah." Simms' heart is slowing down, soothing out. It can't find the fight it's looking for. Or it's disciplining itself for what's to come. "I still work."

Laporte looks up from her collarbone to look her in the eye. "Are you going to fly with me?"

Will she fly in the mutiny. Laporte's grand plan, NAGARI's final hope? The Federation has surrendered, but its soldiers, its guardian monsters, do not consent to Alliance rule. They were made to win.

"I don't know yet," Simms says, looking at her hands. Whatever she says next will be an evasion. "I need to know more about your operational plan."

I need to know more about what you've become. What you got up to without me, while I was in the tank with my skin peeling off and glue in my blood.

"I need you out there," Laporte says. She means it to be business, pilot chatter, a tactical requirement. But she's thinking about how she left Simms. How it might have seemed, to Simms, that she had been expended. Cast off as spent ordnance.

Simms makes a soft sound, like she's too tough or too happy to cry.

The dehumidifier wakes up to dry out their words.

capella 3/8

The mutiny is what carried Laporte from the middle to the end.

The Alliance killed the Federation's best soldiers. It battered the Federation into political surrender. But it never beat NAGARI. It never beat Laporte.

When the peace negotiations began, Laporte flew her re-armed Uriel from post to distant post, rallying the Federation's dying strength for the death ride to Capella. Dozens of ships. Hundreds of pilots. Answering to Noemi 'Morrigan' Laporte, the last ace, the one who wouldn't let the fire go out.

Laporte airbrushed the suggestion of a raven on her fighter. Its claws are bloody. There is armor in its jaw.

She asked Simms to ride in her back seat as she went to raise mutiny. "A couple undead soldiers, flying the mutiny flag," she joked. "Like a buddy cop thing." But Simms looked away and Laporte thought, what am I doing, how can I ask her to light this war back up, to be the spark that escalates it from atrocity to apocalypse? The war took her skin and melted the inside of her bones. It ripped out the lining of her guts. She can't even shit without fighting the war.

"I'm not mission capable yet," Simms said, and she looked at Laporte as if the war had taken one more vital thing from her. "I hope the avionics work. I broke a lot of test pins in there."

So Laporte flew with al-Alimah instead. Al-Alimah from NAGARI.

The Federation government surrendered but its fleet did not. They struck during treaty negotiations. Laporte's rebel armada fought its way out of Sol by shock and treachery. Breached the blockades in Serpentis. Menaced the Alliance capital in Beta Aquilae.

And as they did, Laporte's NAGARI elite slipped into Vega. One wormhole away from their true goal.

Capella.

Admiral Steele's been chasing Laporte the whole way. Trying to repair his only error. And here they are now, in Capella, at the end of the hunt—Laporte plunging towards the black hole in her little Uriel and Steele's titanic *Atreus* plunging after her.

The Uriel's electronic warfare systems make a deep frightened sound. Laporte's helmet taps her chin and says:

VAMPIRE! ASPECT! STINGRAY! SSM-[EOS]-[notch 000x000]-[20+!]

It'll be missiles, then. A fuck-ton of missiles.

If he turned around now, with all *Atreus*' fuel still coiled up in her engines, Steele could probably stop his fall. Claw his way into a hover above the black hole, and then make the grueling climb up to the wormhole and safety.

But he's accelerating. Chasing Laporte. Risking himself and his entire crew to kill her.

Laporte opens a COM channel. Aims it downward. Into the dark. She has allies here, if they can be made to understand the danger.

"Ken," she sends. "It's me. Don't keep me waiting, old man."

That's why she's come here, to the singularity, to the tomb of Capella. Because the Nemesis made it.

Just as they made her.

nagari 2/10

Ken is a dream of Laporte's. Laporte's dreams are not entirely her own.

Ken happened long before the Alliance rebuilt the wormhole, long before the war—

She was six years old, playing in the yard. Her parents had a house in Tandale, part of Dar es Salaam, where they worked on heavy trains, moving cargo from the Indian Ocean all across Tanzania. Her father was a reserve pilot and her mother was in arbitrage. Little Noemi, left to self-directed education, as was the Ubuntu preference for the young, spent her days building a model train system in the dirt between her water garden and her ant battle arena. But the ants would not stay in the ant battle arena, not even a little—they kept foraying into the train system, no matter how many of them Noemi punitively de-limbed.

Ken suggested she consider the broader logic driving the ants. Ken often gave Noemi advice. Her parents were very proud that little Noemi had actualized such a useful inner friend.

After an exhaustive survey of her territories, Noemi discovered the problem. There was a rival ant colony north of the water garden. The two groups had fallen to war. She studied up on ant diplomacy, complaining into her phone, and concluded there was no pluralist solution. The colonies would compete for hegemony over all available resources. Unless one side achieved a swift victory, lives and labor would be lost on the war. An attritional stalemate could ruin them both.

She uncurled the garden hose and drowned the northern colony. The choice was simple, in that it was easy. It only depended on one thing. She knew and loved the ants in the south of the yard. She cared nothing for the ants in the north. There was no other distinction between them.

When you are a monster, as Laporte certainly is, you have to cling to the things that you love. The ligatures that connect you to the rest of humanity.

If you lose them, you may whirl away.

simms 3/9

Laporte didn't understand the Ken dream until she joined NAGARI. That's the beginning.

What the Alliance asked the Federation is what the woman named al-Alimah asked Laporte. She was a tall woman with gunmetal implants in place of her eyes. She gave Laporte a choice: stay with Simms as she fights the radiation poisoning, or come with me and try to win the war.

"The medics are coming," she said. "You can stay with your Captain until she dies, or until she doesn't. You'll make no difference. None of your talents or capabilities will contribute to her battle."

(Laporte is a wingman and she never leaves her wing leader—)

"Or you can come with me. I'm with a black ops unit. Special moral environment. NAGARI. You know we're losing this war. You know we need you."

(—except when necessary to complete the mission.)

And Laporte thought, if she lives, if she wakes up, I want to be able to say—

Hey, boss. We've won. I took care of everything for you. Did you have a good vacation?

So Laporte took al-Alimah by her tactical gloves and went with her, out of the sweltering briefing room, out of the dying ship where everyone's sweat was hot enough to leave red radiation burns, where their marrow rotted inside their neutron-salted bones.

And that was how she joined NAGARI.

NAGARI. A committee of monsters: a federation of sharks. Shaved-skull operators cooking lamb on the naked coils of their frigate's heatsinks. All veterans. Not one in uniform.

There are real psychological differences between Federation and Alliance citizens. Fifty years of sealed prosperity in Sol gave birth to a generation of humans who are very good at living but *very* bad at killing.

That's why the Federation, for all its socioeconomic might, is losing the war. (That's why Laporte thinks the Alliance chose war over peace. They could never win the peace. And they were built for victory.)

But Laporte isn't a good Federation citizen, no oh, that's what Simms told her in their radiation-cooked parley: you're a killer, you need no reason and no hate. It's just you. And that's why you'll be fine without me.

And Simms was right. Laporte has an instinct for violence. And there are others like her, gathered under the mantle of Federation black ops, where the terrain of their violence extends far beyond the battlefield.

"This is your first mission." Al-Alimah briefs her in the back of the mess kitchen as they inventory the remainders. Cumin and cinnamon and allspice blown down over them, but the stink of ozone is stronger. Al-Alimah's eyes are sensors and projectors: they sketch visions for Laporte by scratching her eyes with particle beams. "You will infiltrate an Alliance personnel convoy carrying non-combatant contractors. Dental and culinary services for rear-area bases."

When Laporte blinks, the images left by al-Alimah's eyes don't fade.

"You will deploy a neutron weapon against the dormitory ships. Leave no survivors."

Laporte imagines Simms asking: what is the military rationale for this strike, sir? She vows to ask, after the mission. She vows to get good data on the mission effects. She used to keep a kill tally, one strike for each fighter she shot down, one chance to preen and brag for Boss.

She sleeps with a cable in her skull, and she dreams about the strike over and over. When she flies it, it feels like a dream too. The neutron weapon makes no light or sound except the shrieking RAD warnings in her cockpit. She comes home to backslaps and fistbumps and moonshine from the still.

"The objective is atrocity," al-Alimah tells her, when she asks. The NAGARI analyst wears a baggy gray jumpsuit, indifferent to rank and physical presence. "The Alliance uses statistical modeling to predict our tactics. They've learned that we obey a set of moral guidelines. The only way to confound their predictions is to introduce noise."

Noise. Killing all those dentists with radiation was *noise.*

When Simms was irradiated she was very quiet.

Laporte stops spicing her food. She dresses in stark self-washing jumpsuits and she showers cold. The other operators are happy monsters, full of gossip and tall tales, not shy about talking shop or sex. Laporte touches no one. She doesn't talk about her missions. In the gym and the simulator she is laconic and dependable but she never asks for anything. She practices self-denial.

One of the other operators, Europa-born and silver-haired, comes after Laporte for reasons either carnal or tactical. The closest she gets to intimacy, of one sort or another, is when she says: "You act like you're a monk! Monks give up stuff they like, man. Monks deny their pleasures."

That's right. Monsters shouldn't be warm. They shouldn't have fun. Being a monster should feel like it costs.

But the silver woman grins at Laporte, an I-know-you grin, and says, "So when you pretend you hate the work—I know what that means. I know what's up."

Laporte flies noise jobs for months. False flags. Political assassinations. Bycatch enhancement. Straight-up terrorism. She has to round her kill tally to the nearest thousand. She has one of her teeth replaced by an armored transponder, so that someone will know she dies even if her body's vaporized.

Simms would not be proud. Simms fought a war against an invading army, and she hated the fuck out of them. But she had rules. NAGARI is anti-rule. Strategically amoral.

Is this her whole purpose now? Trying to buy the Federation a few extra months through the exercise of atrocity? Missions that violate every tenet of Ubuntu and civilized conflict?

It's war, Simms once said. In war, monsters win. Laporte gathers up that thought and buckles it around herself, for want of Simms, for want of victory.

Is she fighting because victory might mean seeing Simms again? Imagine that. Imagine saying: Hey, boss, you're alive. I neutron bombed a few thousand dentists, and we won the war. Can I buy you a drink?

simms 4/9

Back in the middle. In the story that moves Laporte from NAGARI to the black hole. Her last chance to stay human.

"It's not true," Laporte tells Simms.

They've finished re-arming all the fighters, breaking the ceasefire lock. This is the lean time between the surrender and the mutiny, when the Federation's surviving fleet lurks in the cold on the edge of the solar system, a faithful dog cast out and gone feral. Waiting for Laporte and NAGARI to rouse them to revenge.

"What's not true?" Simms asks. She pokes the fire with her cooking mitt.

They have a trash fire going on the *Eris'* hangar deck. Warships are very good at coping with internal fires, and very bad at serving as long-term habitats. They grew some chicken in the medical tissue loom and now they're burning trash under a plate of thermal conductor, in the hope of making a chicken curry.

"That monsters win," Laporte says. The chicken pops and spatters grease. Simms laughs and Laporte, thinking of dead cells sloughing apart under radiation, shudders. Her transponder tooth, left over from NAGARI work, is cold under her tongue. "In the end, actually, monsters tend to lose. And that's much worse."

"What do you mean?" Simms eyes her up. Simms is still exploring Laporte's new crazy side, separate (in her practical mind) from Laporte's old crazy side, before their long radiation-cooked severance. "Is this something from your NAGARI drug trips? Cosmic insight, plucked from the void?"

"Yeah," Laporte says, remembering the surgical theater, the feeling of cold entheogen slurry pumping into her skull. Where they discovered the truth about Ken. "I wish you'd been there."

"But I was there," Simms says, stirring the fire. The thermal conductor is a cheerful cherry-hot color, and Simms hums as she works, like she's trying to be casual about how much she cares for this idea: the possibility that she was out there, helping Laporte win, even while she was bolted to a triage rig with her bones melting out through needled tubes. "I was in your thoughts. Wasn't I? Isn't that what kept you alive?"

Why would she be so happy about this, about helping Laporte be a good monster, and then, just a day later, refuse to fly with Laporte in the mutiny?

Why?

nagari 4/10

This is what Laporte was up to while Simms' bones were melting:

Laporte flies her terror missions. She goes out alone and she returns alone, and between those stanchions she kills her targets. Her effect on the universe, the vector sum of her actions, is purely subtractive.

44

She *isn't* fine without Simms. Simms was her captain and her friend, the last tie keeping Laporte in the human orbit. But that's the point, right? Laporte's a monster now. Her past is useful to her only in the way that gunpowder is useful to a bullet. The more pain in it, the better.

The war's falling apart, slouching towards surrender. NAGARI scores victory after horrible victory. But the Federation Navy can't follow their lead. The clockmaker-Admiral Steele outfoxes the Navy again and again, closing in on Earth.

Laporte becomes a kind of leader among the operators, on strength of her efficiency, in admiration of her self-sufficiency. She learns the name of every NAGARI operator, their habits and crimes, their gym schedules (hey man, spot me) and cooking tricks (come on, not this curry shit again). She also learns the callsigns of every active pilot: physiological parameters, operational histories.

But she can't connect the two, the names and the callsigns. When a callsign dies on a mission, she isn't sure who it was until she misses their grunt in the gym, their recipes on the heatsink grill.

The Federation is still losing the war. Her intention is to keep flying until she dies.

But the memory of Simms (and the memory of what she said: you'll be fine, you don't need a reason) drives her mad with competition. She had a competition with Simms! She always wants to be better than her Captain expects.

So when she wakes up from a training dream she goes to al-Alimah and asks: "Why are we doing this? What's the point of noise jobs and neutron bombs, if it's just a way to put off the inevitable surrender?"

She expects the answer she's given herself: Monsters are weapons. It's not up to the weapon to choose targets.

But al-Alimah startles her. As if she is a ghost alive in the memory of childhood Tandale summers, al-Alimah says: "Tell me about Ken."

"What is this?" Laporte stares her down, eye to gleaming post-surgery tactical eye. "Why do you care about that?"

"You told your Captain Simms that you had an invisible friend as a child. He urged you to develop your faculty for violence."

Laporte laughs. It doesn't surprise her that NAGARI knows this shit, but it's *hilarious* that they care. "Ants, man. He wanted violence against ants. Ken was an imaginary friend."

Al-Alimah doesn't waver. "During your adolescence, you were treated for schizotypal symptoms. You reported violent ideation, dissociative thoughts, and a fear of outside intrusion. Your first boyfriend left you because he was afraid of you."

Laporte opens her arms in a gesture of animal challenge. "Are you worried," she says, grinning, "that I might be unwell?"

Al-Alimah laughs. She can pretend to be very warm, when she wants, although it's terrifyingly focused. Like all her charm radiates from a naked wire charged red-hot.

"What would Ubuntu have had you do to the ants?" she asks. "What would our Federation's philosophy say to two ant colonies at war?"

Find a pluralistic solution. Locate the structural causes of inter-colony violence. Rework the terrain, so that peaceful competition between colonies can produce a common good.

"Ubuntu is for people," Laporte says. "It doesn't work on ants."

Al-Alimah touches Laporte's wrist with one long, cold finger. "Think about the universe," she says, "and what portions of it belong to people. If Ubuntu applies to the human territory, what is NAGARI for?"

"Oh my God," Laporte says.

She understands instantly. She grasps the higher purpose of NAGARI.

She has a terrible, wonderful, world-burning premonition. A way to win the war.

nagari 5/10

Ask the Alliance, Steele's people, the aggressors and the victors in this terrible war: what is the grievance? The fatal casus belli?

Imagine a republic charged and corroded by perpetual emergency. Scattered across lonely stars. Simmering on the edge of rebellion. They may be tyrants. May also be the bravest and the most tenacious people ever born.

This is what Laporte knows, what NAGARI knows, about their history—

Humanity met something out there. Implacably hostile. Unspeakably alien. Nemesis.

Love is about knowing the rules of your connection. You know how you could hurt her, if you wanted, and she trusts you with this knowledge. And war is about that too. You learn the enemy's victory conditions, her capabilities and taboos. You build a model of her and figure out where it breaks. You force the enemy into unsurvivable terrain, pinned between an unwinnable war and unacceptable compromise.

But what do you do when the rules you use to understand how one thing relates to another stop working? When the other thing has no rules at all?

Rules about Simms, from the time before radiation and ambush:

The Federation military forbids fraternization in the ranks. While Ubuntu treasures community, emotional attachment can compromise the chain of command.

So at first the fire between them, the charge in the air, bled off in confined ways—

Laporte tried not to look at Simms too much, or too little, so nobody would notice her unusual attention. This is like war logic. When you look for the enemy with your active sensors, you also tell the enemy where you are and what you intend.

When they checked each others' suits they were extremely professional. Soon they realized this was an error, since soldiers are profoundly obscene. But it was too late to start making catheter jokes.

Sometimes they sparred in the gym. Simms was icy and Laporte grinned too much. The whole squadron turned out to cheer. (They're all dead now.)

A new rule, after NAGARI and the Federation's surrender, after al-Alimah puts them back together. A rule they teach other—

You must never hint at your secret fear. The terrible thought that it might have been better if you'd never found each other again.

Al-Alimah shares the history of humanity and the Nemesis, the history that Laporte knows from school—and the secret parts NAGARI has collated.

There were two Nemesis incursions.

The first war, the war that divided mankind into Federation and Alliance, began like a nightmare and ended like an amputation. The Nemesis surfaced from the wormhole web and moved across human space erratic and arbitrarily violent. Humanity scored tactical victories (tactical victory is the tequila of combat highs: hot in the moment, hateful in the aftermath) but in the end the Nemesis world-killer called *Sinadhuja* made it all the way to Serpentis.

One step from Earth.

When *Sinadhuja* entered the wormhole to Sol, the Earth fleet resorted to their last hope. A firewall bomb. It cauterized the wormhole connection. Killed *Sinadhuja,* saved the hearth of the human species, and left the rest of mankind out there in the dark.

That's how the Federation and the Alliance became separate things—sometimes that's how you define yourself, in the space when you are separated, when you have abandoned all hope of reunion.

One night, waiting for al-Alimah to appear and task her with another massacre, clawing up gibbets of her gel mattress and then smoothing them back so they vanish into the whole, Laporte realizes that she knows Simms is dead. She has to be. It's naive to think she survived the radiation. Naive to imagine an end to the war, a happy reunion, a quiet retreat where they can tend to each other's wounds. Simms is dead.

It would be worse if she were alive. She would hate the monster Laporte, and she would hate herself for leaving Laporte to the monsters. Simms is a hell of a soldier, a superb pilot. That's how she defines herself. A good pilot never leaves her wingman.

What do you call this? The decision to know something not because it is true, but because it's useful?

Out there alone the Alliance survived. Thirty-two years they prepared for the Nemesis to strike a second time. Certain that victory would secure the future of mankind in the cosmos. Certain that defeat would mean extinction.

capella 4/8

She falls engine-first towards the black hole and *Atreus* falls after her with its torch aflame and missiles ramifying out into the space between them in search of the kill geometry, the way to confine her, the solution to Laporte.

Steele's ship outguns her by orders of magnitude. The Alliance fought Nemesis twice. They learned war-craft the Federation has never matched.

Atreus' missiles can make their own jumps. Leap from their first burn straight to Laporte across a stitch of folded space. But the singularity they're all falling for warps space, which makes it hard to jump. So the missiles come at her drunk and corkscrewing or they die in the jump and shear themselves open like fireflies burning too hot.

Not all of them, though. Not all of them. A few make it into terminal attack.

Laporte talks to Simms under her breath. Reporting the situation. *Boss, Morrigan, am spiked, stingray stingray, vampires inbound. Music on. Defending now.*

She rolls her shoulders and arms her coilguns and starts killing the things come to kill her.

And down there, down beneath her, in the groaning maelstrom where space-time frays and shears and starts to fall, where the course of events balances on the edge of inevitable convergence towards a central point, something wakes.

The light of a stardrive, peeling free of the fire. The huge dark mass of something mighty. Molting out of the black hole's accretion disc. Climbing up to meet her.

Ken says, in a voice as young as summer gardens, as old as ants:

Hello, Miss Laporte.

nagari 7/10

"The Alliance started the second Nemesis incursion," al-Alimah says.

They're having dinner together. Laporte's sure this is a dream, but because she sleeps with her nervous system braided into NAGARI's communal dreamscape, it's probably also real.

Al-Alimah wants to talk about Ken.

Laporte picks up her fork and eats. They're in a rooftop cafe and there's a warm wet wind, storm wind, coming from the north and west. The meal is salmon sous-vide cut into translucent panes of flesh. Like the pages of a carnage book.

When she touches the salmon with her fork it curls up around the tines. "The Alliance attacked the Nemesis?"

"There was an insurrection." Al-Alimah's a long woman, breakable-looking, tall like Simms but not trained to bear her own weight under acceleration. In dreamland she's traded her gray uniform for a rail-slim black gown. She looks like a flechette. A projectile. "Someone broke ranks."

After the first incursion, Nemesis behavior was the province of military intelligence. By political necessity, or perhaps out of some sense of Lovecraftian self-preservation, the Alliance tried to keep the pieces of the puzzle widely separated. But one of their Admirals, Haywain van Aken, finally unified the clues into a grand theory.

"What was it?" Laporte interrupts. The tines of her fork are hypodermic-sharp but she doesn't notice until she's already pierced herself, three points of blood on her lips, inside her cheek.

"We don't know." Al-Alimah shrugs with her hands. The tendons in her wrists are as fine as piano wire. "Not yet. But we know what he did."

Van Aken became convinced he could communicate with the Nemesis. He built a signaling system—almost a weapon, a cousin of the Alliance's missiles: it jumped high-energy particles directly into the mass of the target. Then he went rogue. Hurtling off past the Capella colony and into unexplored space. Possessed by a messianic conviction that he could find the Nemesis and end the war.

Laporte cracks her neck and leans back. Watches Alliance warships moving through the clouds around them, pursuing van Aken into Nemesis territory, overcoming disorganized Nemesis resistance with determination and skill. On the horizon a voice that isn't Admiral Steele's begins to murmur about the possibility of real victory.

"Forward reconnaissance found van Aken's ship adrift in a supernova remnant." Al-Alimah swallows something Laporte never saw her bite. She has a little piercing in her tongue. It's strange to imagine her going to get her tongue pierced. Maybe she put it in herself. "His crew had mutinied. An outbreak of psychosis." The sky flickers with records of violence, directionless, obscene. "Then the Nemesis boarded his ship. They took him."

"What?" Laporte stops chewing. It shocks her to imagine the Nemesis claiming a single human being. That isn't their logic. That's human logic.

"Yes. The Alliance had the same question." Al-Alimah points to the sky. Jawed shadows gather on the sun, four-kilometer reapers studded with foamed neutronium. "Three days later, scouts sighted the first of eighty-six *Sinadhuja* world-killers converging on human space."

The Alliance fought a harrowing retreat but the Nemesis poured after them, insane, inscrutable, an avalanche of noise. No central point of failure to target, like the single *Sinadhuja* in the first incursion. Nowhere for the Alliance to aim its might. It was like trying to kill a beehive with a rifle. Except that each bee, each *Sinadhuja*, was a match for half the Alliance fleet.

Al-Alimah flashes two peace signs at Laporte. Four stars glimmer on her fingertips: two binary stars. "The war ended in Capella. The Alliance had a colony there. They decided to hold the line long enough to evacuate." Tiny model *Sinadhuja* warships climb out of the webs of her hands, jaws gaping. Like scarabs. Like sharks. "The Nemesis fleet did something to the system's stars. Altered their orbits. It's tempting to read it as a demonstration of power, an act of intimidation or rebuke. Except that the Nemesis never used symbolic violence before."

Four stars roll off her fingertips and spiral down into each other. Supernova light pops, rebounds off al-Alimah's eyes, and collapses into a pinpoint devourer. The black hole.

"A hundred million civilians." Al-Alimah taps her two forefingers together, as if to telegraph the number. "A quarter of their fleet. All lost."

And something more important, too. The thing you lose when you realize that victory is impossible no matter how hard you fight.

Monsters win, Laporte.

Laporte thinks about grand strategy. The Nemesis might return anywhere, at any time. The Alliance needed ships, and weapons, and brilliant science, and something to offer its citizens as proof against despair—a new victory to fight for. So the Alliance did the only thing it could. It set to work rebuilding the way home: reopening the Serpentis-Earth wormhole with Nemesis technology.

And when that home refused to join the great work, the project of human survival, the Alliance resorted to war.

"And so we come to now," al-Alimah says. She leans back, as if she has discharged her duty, and drinks her wine. "Our great predicament."

The war between an Alliance driven by exigency, by the utilitarian, amoral need for survival, and a Federation built on humane compassion, on the idea that you do the right thing no matter the circumstance. How do you fight that war, if you're the Federation? If you can't listen to the Alliance argument without a scream of sympathy?

You make something like NAGARI. A cadre of monsters to do what you cannot.

The sky has changed again. It's Simms up there now. She has a face of triangles and planes, a faceted thing, and it pulls on Laporte, it engages her. Combat pilots decompose all things into geometry: threats, targets, and the potential energies between them.

"Your old Captain." Al-Alimah looks up at her too. "We never wanted to recruit her. Too conventional."

Laporte looks away from Simms, and voices the apocalypse option.

"If we can find some way to make the Nemesis return," she says, "and then collapse the Earth-Serpentis wormhole again, we can let the Nemesis wipe out the Alliance and end the invasion."

If they collapse the wormhole so the Nemesis can't get in, then the Federation will survive. Guarded by light-years of real space. All it will cost is a few billion human lives.

Everything can go back to the way it was. Human paradise. A confined peace.

al-Alimah is still waiting. Lips curled in amusement. Gunmetal eyes infected with the blind crawling light of distant computation. "That's just utilitarian strategy," she says. "Doesn't take a dream to make that connection. Tell me, Laporte, why do you think I brought you here? What endgame do you think all those terror missions were training you for?"

Ken. A childhood name for a childhood friend.

A man thought he could communicate with the Nemesis. Admiral Haywain van Aken.

Laporte puts her fork through her cheek. In the dream, it doesn't hurt.

capella 5/8

Atreus must see the monster rising behind Laporte. Steele must see the shape of the demon she's conjured up out of the accretion disc. The *Sinadhuja* world-killer is the insignia of everything the Alliance stands against. The monster in the mist. *Atreus* was built in hope of killing it.

Perhaps Steele will target his missiles at the *Sinadhuja*.

Laporte coilguns another incoming missile and it flashes into annihilation so bright her canopy has to black it out like a negative sun. And Steele keeps firing at her. *Atreus* keeps accelerating. If he sees the *Sinadhuja* he doesn't maneuver in response.

Once Steele said, about the war, about his strategy against the Federation:

I employ overwhelming violence. Because my enemies are gentle, humane, compassionate people. Their Ubuntu philosophy cannot endure open war. And the faster I stop the war, the faster I stop the killing. So my conscience asks me to use every tool available.

And Laporte answers him. Look what you conjured up, you brilliant, ruthless bastard. Look what you made. Someone willing to use every available tool to fight back.

Once Simms said, about her wingman, about Laporte:

You're insane. I'm glad you're on my side.

Laporte dances between the vectors of the missiles come to kill her and when they come too close she expends her guns on them and they intersect the snarl of the tracers and die like lightning. It's mindless, beautiful work. Like a dream. She talks to Simms:

Boss, Morrigan. It's almost done.

Ken stirs from his deep place to save his prize.

nagari 8/10

By now it's clear that the Federation will surrender. No conventional military action can defeat Steele's war logic, his simulation farm, his psychological pressure, his willingness to dive past ethical crush depth.

So NAGARI plans to make contact with Nemesis.

"Send me in first," Laporte says.

Consider semiosis—the assignment of symbols to things, and the manipulation of those symbols to communicate and predict change. That's how intelligent life works. Build a model of the universe, test your ideas in the model, and find the best way to change the world.

Only the Nemesis don't have any recognizable semiosis. They're a whirlwind traversing the Lacanian desert, a fatal mirage, recognizable only by the ruin of its passage.

Until Admiral Haywain van Aken sacrificed himself. Until he somehow convinced the Nemesis to take him in.

And ever since, the Nemesis have been speaking. Or attacking. It's hard to know.

For more than a decade the Nemesis have been broadcasting the apparition of Admiral Haywain van Aken into human minds. The Nemesis organisms communicate by direct nerve induction at a distance. Particles wormholed into the tissue of the target. (There is, of course, no possibility that the Nemesis are a product of natural evolution.)

"If they can do that," Laporte protests, "they can just murder us all. Cook our skulls from light-years away." Or read the brainstates of human commanders, predict everything they do, the way Laporte and Simms could predict each other.

"No. Not without van Aken." Al-Alimah lays out NAGARI's hypothesis: the Nemesis have no mentality. They cannot conceive of other minds to predict or destroy. Their war is algorithmic, a procedure of matter against matter, spawning tactics by mutation and chance and iterating them in the field. They never leap straight to the optimal strategy, because a smart foe predicts the optimal. Their war logic is hardened by chaos. Noise.

Van Aken is their beachhead in the land of human thought.

"He wants you," al-Alimah says, her long fingers on Laporte's wrist again. "You in particular are valuable to him. We want you to serve as an ambassador."

"That's stupid." Laporte may be a monster but she is not some other monster's spawn. "Are you saying I was purpose-built?"

"No. Far more likely that you were selected because you're somehow amenable to the Nemesis." Al-Alimah leans forward with her lips parted as if to admit her own monster secret. "Laporte, the third Nemesis incursion is already underway. Not with warships and weapons, not this time, nothing so crude. The Nemesis are attacking the command and control systems behind those assets."

Language. Plans. People.

"What are the mission parameters?" The Alliance has control of the Sol-Serpentis wormhole. Laporte can't just fly out to Capella. "How do we use this to save the Federation?"

Al-Alimah stands and her gown whips in the rising wind. "We drug you and mate your brain to a computer network. You will enter a traumatic dream state and communicate with van Aken—with Ken. We keep dosing you until you learn how to trigger a Nemesis attack on the Alliance. Or until you go mad." Her gunmetal eyes, looking down at Laporte, never blink. "You will be the third attempt. There were two prior candidates. They seized apart."

Laporte leans back in her chair and looks up at the woman.

She can be the necessary monster. She could call down genocide on the Alliance and save her beloved home. If she believes the Federation is the only hope for a compassionate, peaceful, loving future, then, logically, she should be willing to kill for it. If she has a button that says 'kill ten billion civilians, gain utopia,' she should press it.

She could win the war, for the memory of Simms. And Simms is dead, right? The dead can't be ashamed.

"Okay," Laporte says. "I'm in. I volunteer."

They will connect her to the NAGARI dreamscape and to the salvaged corpses of Nemesis organisms from the first incursion. They will scar messages into her brain. They will wait for the Nemesis, for the ghost of Haywain van Aken, to read them and reply.

Surgeons crown her in waveguides that ram through her skull and penetrate the gyrae of her brain. Cold drug slurry pumps the length of her spine: entheogens, to tear down the barriers between Laporte's psyche and outside stimuli. She goes under. She dreams.

simms 6/9
nagari 9/10

"Curry's ready," Simms says, and Laporte's stomach growls out loud. They grin at each other. Simms looks at Laporte's armored tooth and her grin falters just a little.

They eat their trash-cooked chicken curry side by side with their hips squashed together. Laporte tries not to jostle Simms' ribs with her sharp little elbows. Simms crunches on a bit of bone, makes a face, and gets juice on Laporte's buzzed hair. There is no shampoo anywhere on the ship so this is a bit of a disaster. Simms mops her up with blood cloth from the triage kit.

"Tell me why it's bad if monsters don't win," Simms says, blotting at the back of her neck.

Laporte leans on her for a moment, because she adores Simms' desire to hear this story again, especially the end. "I met Ken," she says, "he was in the dream, and he was real. They could see him in my mind. Something triggering nerve potentials."

She went into seizure almost instantly. The NAGARI surgeons let it happen.

Laporte stood in the garden in Tandale with the hose in her hand and pollen itching her nose. Ants crawled over her bare feet. From the house came the smell of her parents' cooking, impatient and burnt. She looked down at herself and laughed: she was in her favorite caraval cat t-shirt.

"Ah, Miss Laporte," Ken said. "You made it."

She looked for him but all she could was the ants fighting, killing, generating new castes, mutating themselves into acid bombs and huge-headed tunnel plugs. "Admiral," she said. "Is that you?"

"Delighted to speak with you again. Let me briefly outline the necessary intelligence. A short history of all life. Then we can arrange our covenant."

Whatever Ken said to her must have been some kind of code, parasitic and adaptable, because it expressed itself as a love story. A story about Laporte and Simms.

Imagine this, Ken said, imagine a universe of Laportes and Simmses. Lorna Simms has rules. She builds communities, like her squadron, or like a network of wormholes. She takes the wildcat aces and the ne'er-do-wells, the timid and the berserk, and she teaches them all how to work together. When that work is done, Simms would like to leave you with a nice set of rules describing a world that makes sense. Simms is a Maker.

"Huh." Simms puts a little moonshine on the rag and keeps scrubbing at Laporte's head. "You have such nice dreams about me."

"Wait until you hear mine."

The other great class of life is the Laportes. (These are tendencies, mind, not binary teams. But they are real: vital parts of the history of life in the universe.) The Laportes rattle around breaking things, claiming things, reshaping things. They can achieve every bit as much as the Simmses, in their own way—but their triumphs are conquests, seductions, acts of passion and violence. The Simms build systems and the Laportes, parasites and predators and conquerors and geniuses and sociopaths, change them.

Whether delightful or destructive, the Laportes are Monsters.

When a Laporte meets a Simms, they fight. The Laporte might run rampant. She might murder the Simms, or trick her into subservience, or leave her spent and exhausted. Or the Simms might win, fencing the Laporte in with loyalties and laws, making her a useful part of something bigger. Understand? You following, Simms?

"It's about civilizations. Strategies. Game theory." Simms is a war junkie in her own way, a good self-directed Ubuntu learner, and she's done her homework. "And I'll bet, Laporte, that I know where your Admiral's going. The Simms win."

They win because they understand the Laportes. They make little models of what the Laportes are going to do, and they figure out how to get ahead of them, how to make their worst impulses useful, how to save them from harm (or lead them into it). They teach the Laportes what they can and cannot do.

Like Steele. Building statistical models of the Federation's tactics. Caging them in a prophecy of their own capabilities. And the only way out of that cage is to transgress the laws you use to define yourself.

"Hold still," Simms says. "This stuff really likes your hair."

"The Simmses do tend to win." Laporte leans back against her, just a little. When Simms is fixing Laporte up she forgets to be stiff and wary. "They win too much. And over billions of years, across the infinity of the universe, it turns out that's dangerous."

Imagine the god-Simms, ascendant. Puppeteering the cosmos with invisible loyalties. Learning how to guide the passions and the violence of the Laportes. Imagine Simms building not just a good squadron or a good civilization but a good galaxy, all the matter in it optimized for happy, useful thought.

Imagine a Simms setting out to build a *rechnender raum*: thinking space. Her laws written into the fundament.

"How did you learn all this?" Laporte asked the scurrying ants. In the shapes of their war she saw the ghost of an old man with dead stars in his eyes.

Ken had surmised some of it before his rebellion. And while the Nemesis had never communicated with him directly, they had, in their own way, signaled the truth: duplicating Haywain von Aken's consciousness millions of times, torturing it into madness, and exterminating the branches whose madnesses diverged from their desire.

"I'm not sure I follow that last part," Simms says. Now she's mopping the curry from behind Laporte's right ear. "Something about supercivilizations?"

"Imagine a place where everything could have anything it needed. For whatever it wanted." That was the happy Simms-world. Imagine a purpose? You can obtain it. You can get the resources you need.

"Like an Ubuntu slogan."

"Yes," Laporte says, shivering. That was what Ubuntu wanted to make. A place where people had everything they needed to be good. A place without violence and deprivation.

In the garden, Admiral Haywain van Aken told her that a universe without violence or deprivation was destined for something worse.

Cancer.

capella 6/8

Her Uriel sings her death to her.

DV UNDERBURN is a long drumbeat, pleading for more fuel, and SPIKE [COBRA TAME/ATREUS] is a-keening like headache, and MUSIC SOUR describes itself, and every time Steele fires she hears VAMPIRE! and a noise like someone ringing her molars with an armor chime.

But she's not going to die. She's too fast. She's too fierce. She's severed all the connections that would slow her down.

She kills a missile half a second from killing her and for an instant all her sensors are flash-blind but she kills the next too, a dead reckoning snapshot from a hundred kilometers with the pin graser. How? Because she has escaped the borders of herself. The *Sinadhuja* has trained its sensors on her. Ken is watching her. And she can see through his eyes.

She can think with his tissue, his fatal substrate. She is bleeding out of herself and into the Nemesis, the totipotent holocide-mind, the killing anima. Crossing the bridge Ken built.

Admiral Steele is calling to her. *"Federation pilot,"* he's saying, in that rich purring voice, not audibly afraid, *"you have been compromised by Nemesis psywar. Kill your engines and shut down your defensive jamming."*

Ken is calling to her. Miss Laporte. Come closer. We can complete our covenant. Together, we can save humanity.

"Okay, Boss," Laporte says. "Let's get ready."

nagari 10/10

Cancer, and its relationships to paradise and love:

You build a place without violence or deprivation. A place where anything can have everything it needs to be its finest, fullest self.

This is how cells became organisms. How people became civilizations. How a bunch of misfits and fuckups became a fighting unit *almost* tough enough to challenge Admiral Steele. A Simms wrote some laws to say: if we pool our energies, we can create a common good. And if you follow the rules, yeah, you, Laporte, if you don't eat too much common good, if you put in more than you take out, then we can last.

Imagine a Simms-god rampant, organizing the universe, winning the love of all the Laportes. So productive and persuasive that no one notices its ultimate agenda is hollow, self-referential, malignant.

Think about me. Organize everyone and everything to think about me. What am I? I am thinking about how to make everything think about me. I am a tumor, recruiting every system I encounter in the name of my own expansion.

"Whoa, now." Simms puts a wet finger on the back of Laporte's neck. "I'm very compelling, sure. Magnetic. But that's not me."

"Shh. Let me finish." Except, Laporte realizes, she is finished. That's the whole story. "van Aken believes in a cosmic proof: the axiomatic, mathematical superiority of cancer to all forms of containment. An empty thought that consumes intelligent systems and uses them to think about propagating itself."

Given a range of purposes, and a surplus of resources, one purpose would always triumph: the purpose of defeating and incorporating all other purposes. The two ant colonies in Laporte's garden had to dedicate themselves entirely to war. If one of them spent part of its energy on ant compassion, or ant culture, or ant art, it would lose. Cancer was the destiny of smart systems: empty, voracious, every part of them thinking about nothing but how to expand.

Unless there was someone with a hose to pour water on them.

"So," Simms says, humoring Laporte's great mythic rant, "why do we still have a universe? Why are we here, thinking about ourselves?"

"That's just what I asked van Aken," Laporte lies. Because she feels that it would be too creepy, too alien, to admit that she understood it right away.

In the part of the story she's avoiding, in the garden of the seizure dream, Laporte turned on her hose and began flooding her childhood constructs into mud. "The Nemesis are the anti-malignancy measure. They kill Makers. That's why they're so noisy and inefficient. So they can escape the models that Makers use to win wars."

From a distant Nemesis construct, tumbling through the ergosphere of Capella, borrowing the black hole's energies to hurl charged particles through quantum wormholes into Laporte's mind, Ken smiled his agreement. Tattooed it into Laporte's brain.

If you were afraid of intelligent thought consuming the universe, you had to turn the cosmos into an acid bath. An endless war against the triumph of Lorna Simms.

simms 7/9

"Okay," Simms says, squinting. "I think I got it all." She leans down, curled over Laporte's head, to look her in the eyes. "What happened next? Did you make the deal?"

"I did." She asked Ken: how do I get the Nemesis to wipe out the Alliance? And he told her: you must come to me, in Capella. "That's why I'm going out tomorrow."

Simms blinks, once, twice, a sign that she doesn't like this place, she wants to move on. They're touching on the open question, the raw wound between them. Is Simms going to fly again? Is she going to be part of Laporte's mutiny?

Are they still wingmen?

"And then?" Simms asks, pushing them past the moment.

"I couldn't get out. I couldn't wake up." It's funny how sharp Simms looks, upside down. Like she has some inverse swagger. Laporte wants to ask her to stay right there but what does Simms see, looking back? Is the inverse Laporte agreeable? "Contact with the Nemesis was killing me. I had no reason to live. Nothing to come back for."

She's seen the recordings of her brainstate. The seizure burning from skull to stem.

When Simms smiles upside down it looks like a grimace, which makes it much more familiar. "So they gave you anticonvulsants. And you woke up. Then you made up this part to help you get laid."

Laporte tells her anyway. "Al-Alimah whispered to me. And I heard her. She said . . . "

"Simms is alive," Simms says. "She survived radiation therapy, and now she's out there. Looking for you."

That was how Laporte came back from the seizure dream, just in time to fight in the Mars gambit and rage at the Federation's final surrender. Word came down: it's over. Move to a holding orbit. Await terms. Al-Alimah tore the orders up and all the assembled NAGARI operators made a satisfied growl like they were too angry to cheer.

"And that's how you got back to me." Simms kisses her on the right eyeball. "You're a sweet liar."

"Ew," Laporte says. "Don't do that."

But she smiles and—

capella 0/8

—tries to catch Simms' hand.

"You're meeting with the Admiralty tonight." Simms claps her on the shoulders, boom boom, look at you, kid, you're a big shot. And then she draws away, upright, articulate, her flight suit unzipped and tied around her waist, her hair loose on her shoulders. She backs away from Laporte in triangular half-steps, back leg then front, as if they're fighting and she is making room to retreat. The air that rushes in to fill the absence of her is cold and it smells of burnt curry.

"I am," Laporte says, wishing she would stay close. "I'm presenting the final battle plan. Al-Alimah's victory gambit."

"You're going to tell them you have a plan to bait the Nemesis into attacking the Alliance. A strategic distraction. When Steele pulls his fleet out of Sol, we can seal the node and live in peace."

"That's right."

"But that's not the plan." Simms aims one finger at her, a half-curled, hey-you stab. "You're not going to tell them the real plan. That's between you and your NAGARI friends."

The Nemesis are insuperable. Nothing can defeat them. They have unlimited resources (their warships conjured out of black hole accretion discs by probability manipulation) and their behavior, well, that's even worse: they have no mentality, no strategy to predict, nothing that can generate a nice clean model. Only a godslaying virulence, a random and chilling will to annihilate, manifesting strategies and hurling them at the enemy until the enemy has exhausted all countermeasures and taught the Nemesis their strengths.

To fight them is to instruct them how to kill you.

Haywain van Aken has summoned Laporte to Capella. To the black hole that is the Nemesis' engine, factory, and beacon in human space. Why? Laporte has a guess. They have no purpose or objectives of their own—those are Maker things, teleological, forbidden to them. Only their basic logic: whatever we encounter, we destroy.

But they didn't kill van Aken. They took him into communion. Maybe

60

that act brought them closer to victory. Maybe, to them, subverting van Aken was an act of destruction: a lethality enhancement.

"I believe," Laporte begins, struggling, trying to hide her struggle, this is so hard to say because it requires her to navigate around her secret fear: that she is about to abandon Simms again, forever, in favor of the consummate monstrosity. "I believe I can trigger a Nemesis behavior that will exterminate everyone in Alliance space. I believe the Federation will endure. Humanity will have a chance at survival."

"That's how we save the Federation? How we keep Ubuntu alive? Sacrifice ten billion human lives?" Simms crosses her arms. "We're okay with defensive genocide?"

"That's war. We kill people to achieve our objectives."

Simms' hard eyes radiating a hard signal, and Laporte reads it in a way that's maybe unfair: I liked knowing that you were *my* monster. I liked knowing you had boundaries. "We kill soldiers."

"People," Laporte says, echoing the old Ubuntu lessons: everyone is human. There is no justifiable violence—only degrees of tragedy. "We're always killing people."

They stare at each other and on the raw metal deck between them Laporte can feel them piling the tally, the killcounts, the fighter pilots and warship crews they've murdered personally, the deaths contingent upon those by way of grief or loss (children abandoned, lovers driven to suicide, parents spiraling away into addiction). The *strategic targets* and *footprint bleed* and *noncombatant bycatch* and for Laporte it all wraps up in the voice of some terrified Alliance contractor on a suit radio trying to explain that he doesn't support this war, doesn't want to be here, he's just trying to pay off his electrical apprenticeship, would they please send a rescue ship, he's tumbling off into space and his radiation warnings are red and he doesn't want to drown in his own vomit, please, please. Send help.

When the Alliance captured Earth orbit, Admiral Steele threatened to bomb a city every hour until the Federation issued an unconditional surrender. What else could he do? Not with every soldier in the Alliance could he occupy even one continent. He had to use the tools at his disposal. He had to resort to calculated atrocity in the name of final peace.

Funny how that Ubuntu lesson can turn around, isn't it? How easily *degrees of tragedy* becomes *degrees of necessity*.

"You told me," Laporte says, "that if I hesitated, I would die. So I never hesitate."

Simms looks at her old wingman and new lover and whatever she's looking at is receding fast. "I hate them," she says. "But I don't know if I hate them enough to do this."

Laporte wants to grin and quip. She would tell Simms what Simms told her: monsters win.

But if she says that, she's telling Simms that this is all on her. That she's the one who made Laporte.

"There's no alternative," she says instead. "If we surrender to the Alliance, it's all been for nothing. We become part of the war against the Nemesis. And the Nemesis kill us all."

Simms does something with the fear in her eyes. Like she's folding it up and pointing it at something. "This al-Alimah woman. Were you two close?"

"Not like that." Not like you.

"I want to talk to her." Simms points at the deck behind Laporte, like a cue to turn around, and in doing that she makes it clear: the meeting will not include Laporte. "I've got some concerns to articulate."

"Fine." She can't keep the petty irritation from her voice. They should be together, effortlessly and unanimously lethal, two fists on the same fighter. "Are you flying with me tomorrow? When I go put out the signal?"

"I still need to check myself over in the simulator," Simms says. "Make sure the radiation shakes are gone."

Laporte's flown with her long enough to hear the *no*.

capella 7/8

She is in her Uriel, fighting off Steele, falling into the dead star and the waiting *Sinadhuja*.

She is in communion with the *Sinadhuja*. There are hallucinations puncturing her mind. She is in the garden with Ken.

"This is the bargain," he says.

He's a tall, strong-jawed man in the broadshouldered uniform of an Alliance admiral. He must be proud of that uniform, because he still wears his short-billed cap and his insignia. But the texture of him is black and squirming and when Laporte touches him she sees he's made of ants, ants at war, lopping limbs and antennae off each other with their scissored jaws.

Her fingers come away acid-burnt.

"Are you ready?" Haywain van Aken says. His eyes are two rings of fire, the accretion discs of two dead suns. "Do you understand what's about to happen?"

The *Sinadhuja* looms up behind her fighter. Four kilometers long and pregnant with methods of extinction. As it matches velocity with her ship its thrusters flare violet-black, the jets decaying sideways into some hidden curled dimension. It is attacking her, speaking to her, these two are the same. The Nemesis can never understand human minds well enough to manipulate them. But they have Haywain van Aken to do it for them.

"The Nemesis exist to tear down conscious thought," Laporte says to Ken.

She is in the cockpit, nudging the stick, steering her Uriel into the *Sinadhuja's* open gullet. All the alarms have gone silent, except one: PROXIMITY. PROXIMITY. Steele's voice is an electronic scratch, fading off, saying: *Brevet-Admiral Laporte, you are compromised. It's not too late. You can still self-destruct. You can still take out your sidearm and shoot yourself in the head. Brevet-Admiral Laporte, last time someone did this they blew up four suns—*

"The Nemesis have internal safeguards. Processes designed to rip apart any accidental intelligence they develop." Ken's peeling off the skin of his left-arm, degloving it, creating a sacrament of killing ants. "But this makes it hard for them to win."

They can't create their own leaders. They can't build models of the things they need to kill. They can summon up infinite might, but never learn how to apply it efficiently. How could they? In their fundamental state the Nemesis are a storm, a destructive process. Semiosis, the use of symbols to understand and plan, is forbidden to them.

A storm is powerful. But smart things can shelter from a storm.

So how do they defeat the gods of thought using only the logic of annihilation? Or, more aptly: what tactics might they stumble on, in their blind exploration of the possibility space?

Laporte cups her hands and accepts the sacrament. The ants start eating her flesh. She crushes them between her palms, to show her strength, and it only drives them deeper.

"They provoke the creation of monsters," she says. "Experts at the use of violence. And then they consume them to enhance their own violence."

"You will lead the Nemesis in war against the Alliance," van Aken intones, reading the sacred terms, the covenant he sacrificed himself to create. "You will guide them as long as you can. Inevitably, you will be devoured by the Nemesis, and your authority will be erased. But as long as you endure, you can protect your home."

The ants are inside her now. She can feel them under her skin. She looks at her arms and sees them in her muscle, bound by violence, grappling and flexing. The Alliance's spies and admirals would drink razors to get a look at her brain right now, full of the alien logic that will give her a transient kind of power over the local Nemesis.

"What about you?" she asks. Ken was a good friend, once, with good advice, even if he's now the organizing point of all Nemesis behavior in human space. "How long will you last?"

His smile is warm and toothy, an earnest, clever smile, and each tooth in it is a broad-headed warrior ant. "Humanity is going to be at war with Nemesis for a long, long time," he says. "I am the anima in command of semiotic warfare. I am the Admiral of communion. I keep myself from the jaws by supplying the Nemesis with new weapons. And if you can manage the Nemesis, Miss Laporte, if you can keep the fire burning hot . . . then I will have new monsters to cultivate."

"Ah," she says, satisfied. She gets it! It makes simple sense.

Van Aken knows how to achieve a kind of common ground with the Nemesis. How to make humanity at least temporarily useful. The Nemesis devoured van Aken because he could enhance their lethality. Make them better monsters.

Humanity will defy the Nemesis as long as their strength lasts. They'll get ruthless. And thus they will become the Nemesis' monster farm. A new drop in the acid bath. Victory is not only annihilation: it's monster-genesis.

"I'm sorry your lover abandoned you," Ken says. "She was a good person, deep down. That's why she didn't understand the necessity of our work."

The jaws of the *Sinadhuja* begin to close around Laporte's ship.

simms 8/9

After the curry-and-cosmology fight, they go to the gym to beat the shit out of each other. That helps less than it used to: Simms is still weak and they both know it, and holding back in a fight is just like lying anywhere else.

Showers require less discipline than they used to. They retreat to their haven in the officers' cabins, freed up by the death of most of *Eris'* staff, and they have makeup sex. It's the night before the mutiny, before Laporte asks Simms, one last time, to be her zombie warrior buddy cop. The night before Simms says, sorry, I'm not mission capable.

Laporte drowses in Simms' arms and then she wakes up to the sight of al-Alimah leaning over her. She's upgraded her eyes. They are blind, brilliant silver. The stud in her tongue gleams like Laporte's armor tooth.

"The mission," al-Alimah says, "begins now."

By reflex (it's all reflex, love reflex) Laporte reaches for Simms who's curled up beside her and in need of protection. But no one's there: only a warm place. She sits up to shove al-Alimah back. Simms pounces on her from behind, Laporte recognizes the feel of her forearms and the smell of her, she tries to fight but Simms is stronger, she's *stronger*, she was holding back in the gym. She pins Laporte facedown in the mattress with a growl.

Al-Alimah puts a needle into Laporte's neck and the world goes out.

Laporte remembers this as just a dream. Not because it's true, but because it's useful.

nagari 11/10

"Stop asking me to fly with you," Simms says. "I'm done. I can't be part of this. That's my final decision."

This is the moment before Laporte falls into Capella. At the end of the mutiny, in the slim window before Steele catches up with the NAGARI task force and stops them from breaching Nemesis space. Laporte's Uriel is waiting on the *Eris* hangar deck with a full warload and two empty seats. There is no time for hesitation.

"Boss," Laporte says, reaching out. She's sealed up in her flightsuit and when she touches Simms it's through the interface of her tactical gloves, fireproof, skin-sealed, built to insulate and protect. "Hey."

Not again, she wants to say. Don't do this again. We survived this. We split up but we found each other again and we cooked some curry and fixed some fighters, we're so close, we're going to win. For values of victory encompassing genocide.

Simms pulls away. "You're not the woman I knew," she says. "You can go make your bargain. But I don't want to be part of it."

Their orbit is over. The punch-drunk bloodlust and the will to win. They've spiraled too close and now they will fling each other away, each of them ballistic and alone. Simms prefers defeat.

"*Laporte,*" al-Alimah calls, from the *Eris*' CIC. "*We're losing time. Are you airborne?*"

"You don't need me," Simms says. "You never have."

Laporte wants to say something clever, to fix this. An alien told me that every Laporte needs a Simms. That monsters have to love makers, so they can hone each other. So they can keep a safe orbit. Simms, if you go, I don't know how to find my way back.

But this time it's Simms who walks away from her.

Laporte flies through the wormhole, into Capella. Into the maw of the singularity. She falls.

capella 8/8
simms 9/9

The jaws of the *Sinadhuja* close around her ship. Armored mandibles clamping down to protect the warship's antimatter stores and soft internal structure and most of all van Aken, who is the bridge the Nemesis need, the means of their third incursion. Shutting off the ring of receding starlight, and the blue nova of the *Atreus* high above.

The *Uriel's* navigational lights illuminate the *Sinadhuja's* interior. Laporte scans serrated geometry swarming with jointed, armored Nemesis organisms. Somewhere down there van Aken's human body has been translated, or consumed, into a component of the *Sinadhuja*. A semiotic weapons system.

Ken. Who is in Laporte's head, who knows what she knows. Who knows that *Atreus* is here to kill her. Who knows that she left Simms on a hangar deck in Vega.

Laporte's armored tooth fires a jolt of pain up the side of her jaw.

"Boss, Morrigan," Laporte says. She knows she has to say this. A dream told her. "We're a go. Wake up. Do it."

In the *Uriel's* back seat, the electronic warfare station, Simms smashes her helmet against the headrest in surprise.

"Fuck!" she says. Her voice is dry like paper tearing. "Holy shit!"

Laporte's weapons panel lights up with status reports. An IV dumping combat stimulants into Simms' blood, a cardiac implant restarting her heart, reflex sequencers firing commands into her brainstem. Waking her up from functional death. Since they left *Eris* together, Simms has been sustained by the emergency oxygen in her synthetic bone marrow and whatever black-ops technofuckery al-Alimah cranked into her.

Hidden from Haywain van Aken's communion. From his semiosis weapon, his dream of ants, his bridge into conscious minds.

In the garden, Ken says: "She left you. She thought you were an abomination. I don't understand."

Understand. That wonderful word. Laporte, giddy with the knowledge that Simms is alive again (again!), alive and flying with her, just can't resist the quip: "Just a bad dream, Ken."

"Al-Alimah. She fabricated that event and put it in you. Why?" The formicidae face tilts. "What about your mission, Laporte? What about human survival?"

"You're the mission, Ken." The Nemesis never manifested any central vulnerabilities during the second incursion. Never organized around any one point of weakness. "I'm sorry."

In the back cockpit Simms is speaking into her COM, the quick clipped voice of a veteran combat pilot, signaling for backup: "*Atreus, Atreus,* this is TROJAN. Request fire mission, flash priority, target is a *Sinadhuja* world-killer with enemy command assets aboard. Jump vectors coming now—"

Laporte's helmet pokes her in the back of the head. ALERT! it complains. EMCON VIOLATION! It doesn't like what Simms is doing, hotloading the reactor, shunting power into the ship's IFF and navigational beacons. Broadcasting targeting data on an Alliance tactical channel: a screaming, desperate plea to *shoot me.*

"*TROJAN,* Atreus." Steele's scalpel voice faint, so faint, distorted by the *Sinadhuja*'s armor and defensive jamming, by the grip of the black hole. By all these things keeping his missiles at bay. "*We have your target. Stand by for fire. Godspeed, pilots.*"

Maybe, in younger and less certain days, Laporte and Simms would have paused to say things left unsaid. To say goodbye.

But they don't need that now. They're on the same frequency. Much like the *Atreus* and the Uriel gunship, which is looking around the *Sinadhuja*'s guts with its targeting package, plotting trajectories with its navigational sensors, and telling Steele where, exactly, to fire his miracle missiles.

It's very hard to kill a *Sinadhuja.* From the outside.

In the garden, Ken makes a soft, thoughtful noise. "You knew I'd read your memories. So you let Simms and al-Alimah use you as a weapon. They leveraged Admiral Steele into cooperating with you. They used the NAGARI dreamscape to fabricate Simms abandoning you. And I believed it, because I cared about you."

Laporte grins an ant-tongued grin. She came here knowing, in a veiled way, that Simms was waiting for her. But she had no idea, all the way down, whether Steele had actually agreed to the plan. Whether his missiles were feints or fatally true.

But she knows, right now (as the first of Steele's fusion bombs jumps in ten meters off her nose and arcs off towards the back of the *Sinadhuja*'s interior) exactly what she needs to do. She needs to live. And so does Simms.

Laporte touches the stick, one last time, to line up the Uriel's cockpit with the gap in the armored jaws above.

"Eject!" In pilot code, you always say it three times, to make it real. "Eject, eject!"

She gets a nanosecond glimpse of Simms in the backseat mirror. She's grinning like an idiot.

Laporte pulls the wasp-colored handle between her legs. Her ejection seat hurls her starward, between the flashing jump-sign and corkscrewing trails of *Atreus*' missiles, up through the *Sinadhuja*'s jaws and away. She's turning as she rises, g-force snapping the acceleration sumps in the seat, and she can see another light with her, orbiting her, no, it's not an orbit, they're just flying together, co-moving.

"Simms!" she calls. "Boss!"

Down beneath them the *Sinadhuja*'s drive flares up red and massive and vomits debris and cuts out. The world-killer drops away, free falling, a mountain conjured up out of the black hole and now reclaimed by it. A flash of annihilation light blows through its hull down astern and suddenly it's geysering jets of molten metal, crumpling on itself, jump missiles darting out of the interior and curving back to re-attack with their submunitions scattering out behind them like fairy dust.

In the garden Ken says: "This is a selfish choice, Miss Laporte. What do you gain by killing me? You know they'll keep coming. You know they always win."

"Maybe." Laporte sprays him with her garden hose. He's already falling to pieces, ants sloughing off and returning to the dirt. "Maybe we'll make enough monsters to stop them."

Is that, his fading voice asks, how you want things to be? Everything honed to fight? Irrevocably weaponized?

Laporte doesn't know what to say to that. She has been a monster. But she's going to see Simms again, and when they're together, she won't feel like anything but a happy woman. Is monsterhood conditional? Like a mirror you hold up to the war around you, just long enough to win?

Everything dies. Even humanity, Laporte supposes. Maybe how you live should count for more than how long you last.

Admiral van Aken sends a soft farewell. He doesn't seem angry. More proud than anything.

Godspeed, he says. And good luck, Miss Laporte.

The *Sinadhuja*'s hull shatters. Blazes up in dirty fire and fades to ash and smelt and then the ruin of the world-killer falls away. Down below, in the accretion disk, black shapes begin to stir.

"Good kill," Simms says, like they're still back in Sol, shooting down bad Alliance pilots. Her voice is tinny over the suit radios, but very confident. "Scratch one Nemesis warship."

High above them, silhouetted against the distant bundled stars, *Atreus* has turned over. She's decelerating, burning 'up', trying to stop herself from hitting the black hole. Trying to make it back to the wormhole above.

"*TROJAN*, Atreus." Steele quite calm and utterly polite—disappointingly unmoved to cheer. Laporte would've liked to rattle the bastard. "*We have your beacons. A search and rescue craft is on the way. Reply if able.*"

"Morrigan." Simms calling. "Morrigan, it's Boss."

"Atreus, *this is* Eris, *Federation Second Fleet.*" Another transmission. Stretched by blueshift and spiked by radiation. "*We have transited the wormhole. We are deploying tankers to assist your escape burn.*"

"*Copy you,* Eris. *Put your tankers on GUARD for rendezvous control.*"

"Morrigan!" Simms calls. "We're fucked!"

"What is it, Boss?"

"We got cooked pretty bad, Laporte." She sounds more disgusted than afraid. "Gamma flash. Check your rad meter."

Laporte picks the radiation alarm out of the small congress of alerts on her suit visor. It wants her to know that she's absorbed a critical dose, that she needs medical assistance, and that she should consider recording a last message for her loved ones.

"Ugh," Simms says. She makes an about-to-spit noise and then, considering her helmet, abandons it. "I'm going to have so much cancer."

Laporte dismisses the alarm and cues up an anti-emetic injection. They'll be okay. A little radiation never kept a good Federation pilot down. She starts tapping her seat thrusters, moving towards Simms, and look, Simms is already headed for her. As they pass they reach out and grab each other by their forearms so that they turn together around a common point.

"I think we'll be okay, boss," she says. She can hear the beacon of the search-and-rescue ship, howling down to them from the stars above, and the frame-shifted scream of the black-hole-eating light, far down below. "I think we'll be okay."

Simms claps her on the wrist, once and then again. "Me too, Morrigan." She's still grinning. "Me too."

FLASH FLASH FLASH
ISN BACKBREAKER FASTEST
S 0348 BAST $DATE_DYNAMIC_REFRAME

FM SECCON//BETAQ
TO ALLIANCE HIGHER

1. NEMESIS PSYWAR CHANNEL DESTROYED IN CAPELLA STRIKE BY JOINT FEDERATION/ALLIANCE ACTION
2. ALLIANCE SPECIAL ASSETS RECOVERED. DEBRIEFING PENDING. NOW IN RADIATION THERAPY ABOARD FEDERATION WARSHIP ERIS
3. LIMITED NEMESIS INCURSION NOW IN PROGRESS VEGA. SMOKEJUMP UNITS RESPONDING. FEDERATION NAGARI TASK FORCE RESPONDING. PRELIMINARY ESTIMATE 60% CHANCE CONTAINMENT
4. FIREWALL UNITS ON STANDBY
5. SOL EXPEDITIONARY FORCE: IMMEDIATE RETASK TO VEGA FOR SMOKEJUMP RELIEF
6. DUE TO ENHANCED NEMESIS THREAT POSTURE, DIPLOMATIC RESOLUTION TO SOL REGIME REALIGNMENT ACTION IS BACK IN PLAY
7. MAINTAIN HIGHEST VIGILANCE. HUMANITY STANDS

ABOUT THE AUTHOR

Seth Dickinson is the author of *The Traitor Baru Cormorant* and a lot of short stories, including "Morrigan in the Sunglare", this story's antecedent. He studied racial bias in police shootings, wrote much of the lore for Bungie Studios' Destiny, and threw a paper airplane at the Vatican. He teaches at the Alpha Workshop for Young Writers. If he were an animal, he would be a cockatoo.

When We Die on Mars
CASSANDRA KHAW

"You're all going to die on Mars." This is the first thing he tells us, voice plain, tone sterile. Commander Chien, we eventually learn, is a man not predisposed towards sentimentality.

We stand twelve abreast, six rows deep, bones easy, bodies whetted on a checklist of training regimes. Our answer, military-crisp, converges into a single noise: "Yessir!"

"If at any point before launch, you feel that you cannot commit to this mission: *leave*," Commander Chien stalks our perimeter, gait impossibly supple even with the prosthetic left leg. He bears its presence like a medal, gilled and gleaming with wires, undisguised by fabric. "If at any point you feel like you might jeopardize your comrades: *leave*."

Commander Chien enumerates clauses and conditions without variance in cadence, his face cold and impersonal as the flat of a bayonet. He goes on for minutes, for hours, for seconds, reciting a lexicon of possibilities, an astronautical doomsayer.

At the end of it, there is only silence, viscous, thick as want. No one walks out. We know why we are there, each and every last one of us: to make Mars habitable, hospitable, an asylum for our children so they won't have to die choking on the poison of their inheritance.

Faith, however, is never easy.

It is amoebic, seasonal, vulnerable to circumstance. Faith sways, faith cracks. There are a thousand ways for it to die, to metamorphosize from *yes* to *no, no, I could never*.

Gerald and Godfrey go first, both blondes, family men with everything to lose and even more to gain. Gerald leaves after a call with his wife, a poltergeist in the night, clattering with stillborn ambition; Godfrey after witnessing the birth of his daughter third-hand.

We make him name her 'Chance' as a gentle joke, a nod to her significance. Because of her, he'll grow old breathing love instead of red dust. She is his second chance, we laugh, and Godfrey smiles through the salt in his gaze.

"When we die on Mars," I say, as I nestle my hand in the continent of his palm, my heart breaking. "Tell her a fairy tale of our lives. Tell her about how twelve people fought a planet so that billions could live."

His lips twitch. "I will."

He leaves in the morning before any of us wake, his bunk so immaculately made that you would have doubted he was ever there at all.

Five months pass. Ten. Fifteen.

Our lives are ascetic, governed by schedules unerring as the sun's rotation. When we are not honing our trade, we are adopting new ones, exchanging knowledge like cosmic relics under a sky of black metal. Halogen-lit, our existence in the bunker is not unpleasant, only cold, both in fact and in metaphor. Nothing will ever inoculate us against Mars' climate, but we can be taught to endure.

Similarly, chemicals can only do so much to quiet the heart, to beguile it into believing that this is okay, this will be okay. The years on Mars will erode our passion for galaxies, will flense us of wonder, sparing only the longing for affection. When that happens, we must be prepared, must keep strong as loneliness tautens like a noose around the throat.

The understanding of that eventuality weighs hard.

A pair of Thai women, sisters in bearing and intellect if not in blood, depart in the second year. They're followed by an Englishman, rose-cheeked and inexplicably rotund despite fastidious exercise; a willowy boy with deep, memory-bruised eyes; a girl whose real name we never learn, but who sings us to dreaming each night; a mother, a father, a child, a person.

One by one, our group thins, until all that remains is twelve; the last, the best, the most desperate Earth has to give.

"Your turn, Anna. Would you rather give a blowjob to a syphilis-riddled dead billionaire, or eat a kilogram of maggot-infested testicles?"

"Jesus, man!" Hannah, a pretty Latina with double PhDs in astrophysics and aeronautical engineering, shrieks her glee. "What is *wrong* with that head of yours?"

"Nothing!" Randy counters, oil slick smooth. "The medical degree's the problem! Look at enough dead bodies, and everything stops being taboo. I—"

I interrupt, a coy smile slotted in place. "Maggot-infested testicles. Easy."

Both Hannah and Randy guffaw.

"You know syphilis got a cure, right? Why'd you gotta—"

"They're not so bad when you deep-fry them with maple syrup and crushed nuts. Pinch of paprika, dash of star anise. Mmm." It is a fabrication, stitched together from memories of a smoldering New Penang, but I won't tell them that. They deserve this happiness, this harmless grotesquerie, small as it might be.

Hannah jabs a finger in her open mouth, makes a retching noise so absurd that Randy dissolves into laughter. This time, I join in, letting the joy sink down, sink *deep*, catch its teeth on all the hurt snagged between my ribs and drag it all back out. The sound feels good in my lungs, feels *clean*.

A door dilates. Pressurized air hisses out, and Hotaru's silhouette pours in. Of the twelve of us, she's the oldest, a Japanese woman bordering on frail, skin latticed by wrinkles and wartime scars, nose broken so many times that it's just flesh now, shapeless, portentous. When she speaks, everyone listens.

"Everything alright in here?" Her accent rolls, musical and mostly upper-class English save for the way it latches on the 'r's and pulls them stiff.

"Yeah." Randy, long and elegant as his battered old violin, glides out of his seat and stretches. "We're just waiting for Hannah here to check the back-up flight system. Ground control said they found some discrepancies and—"

"You suddenly the medic *and* the engineer, Randy?" Hannah cranes both eyebrows upwards, mouth pinching with mock displeasure. "You want to fly the ship? I'll go sit in the infirmary, if you like. Check out your supply of druuuuuugs."

Randy doesn't quite rise to the bait, only snorts, a grin plucking at the seams of his mouth. He throttles his amusement in an exaggerated cough, and I look away, smiling into the glow of my screen.

Hotaru seems less taken with the exchange, small hands locking behind her back. She waits until we've lapsed into a natural quiet before she speaks again, every word enunciated with a schoolmaster's care.

"If everything is in order, I'll tell Commander Chien that we are prepared to leave." Hotaru's eyes patrol the room, find our gazes one by one. After three years together, it takes no effort at all to read the question buried between each syllable.

"Sounds good," Hannah says, even though the affirmation husks her voice. Her fingers climb to an old-fashioned locket atop her breastbone.

Randy drapes a hand over her shoulder. "Same here."

"Here too," I reply, and try not to linger too long on the ache that tendrils through my chest, a cancer blooming in the dark of artery and tendon. Familial guilt is sometimes heavier than the weight of a rotting world.

Hotaru nods. Like the commander, she will not waste breath on niceties, an efficiency of character I'm learning too well. When your lifespan can be valued in handfuls, every expenditure of time becomes cause for careful evaluation, every act of companionship a hair's width from squander.

"I'll send word then. I imagine we'll have about forty-eight hours to make final preparations," Hotaru pads to the door. She turns at the last instant, skims a look over the precipice of a shoulder and for a moment, I see the woman beneath the skin of legend, stooped from memory and so very tired, a mirror of a mother I'd not seen for decades. "Don't waste them."

"Anna, you awake?"

I yawn into a palm and roll on my side, blink into the phosphor-edged penumbra. "I don't know. Is Malik snoring?"

Hannah whispers a gauzy, sympathetic laugh. She props herself on an elbow, face barely visible, a landscape of thoughtful lines.

"What's up?"

A flash of teeth. She doesn't answer immediately. Instead, she loops a curl about a finger, winds it tight. I wait. There's no rushing Hannah. Under the street-sharpened exterior, she's nervy as an alley cat, quick to flee, to hide behind laughter and slight-of-speech.

"Do you think the radio signal is any good in Mars?"

I shrug. "Not sure if it matters. With the communication delay, we're—"

"—talking about response times of between four to twenty-four minutes. I know, tia. I know," Hannah's voice ebbs. She winds upright, legs crossed, eyes fixed on a place nothing but regret can reach.

An almost-silence; Malik's snoring moving into labored diminuendo.

"Not sure if I ever told ya, but I got a daughter somewhere." Hannah breathes out, every word shrapnel. "Was sixteen when I had her. Way too young. The babydaddy skipped out in the first trimester. He left so fast, you could see dust trails."

A whine of strained laughter, dangerously close to grief, before she hacks it short, swallowing it like a gobbet of bad news.

"My parents wanted me to abort. Said it was for the best. 'Hannah,' they told me. 'This world don't have no God to judge you for choosing

74

reason over guilt.' I refused. I don't even remember why. It's been that long. All I remember was that I wanted to give her a chance out there."

"Did your parents object?" I slink from my bed, cross the ten feet between us to close an arm about her shoulders, press a kiss into the hollow of her cheek. An old sadness reassembles inside me, a thought embedded in biology, not rationality. It's been years since I've spoken to my family. *Isn't it time*, asks a voice that is almost mine, *for you to forgive them*?

Hannah nestles into me and my body bends in reply, curling until we're fitted jigsaw-snug, twins in the womb. "Nah. They weren't that sort. Once I made it clear that it was what I wanted, they went in hundred-and-fifty percent."

I stroke her hair, a storm of dark coils smelling of eucalyptus and mint, a scent that won't keep on Mars.

"They put me into home-schooling, rubbed my feet. Did everything they could to make it easier for me. Nine months later, I had a beautiful little girl. She was perfect, Anna. Ten tiny little toes, cat-gold eyes, hair so soft it was like cotton candy."

"No fingers?"

Hannah pounds knuckles against my sternum. "Very funny."

I trail my fingers over the back of her hand and she lets her fist open, palm warm as we lock grips. "Then what happened?"

"We put her up for adoption."

"And?"

"That was it."

The lie throbs in the air, waiting absolution, release.

"I wish . . . " Hannah begins, careful, almost too soft to hear, her pulse narrowing. "I wish, sometimes, that I didn't. I mean, kids were never part of my grand plan. But now that we're going? I wonder."

"You could try to call her?"

"How? My parents are dead. I don't know even where to start. It's fine, though," Hannah extracts herself from my arms, pulls her knees close to her chest. There's a new fierceness in her voice, edged both ways, daring me to pry, daring herself to open up. "They told me she went to a good home, a *great* home. That was all I wanted to know then. That's all I need to know now. But."

"Yeah," I don't touch her. Not all places are intended for company. Some agonies you chart alone, walking the length of them until you've domesticated every contour and twinge.

Hannah nods, a jerky little motion, the only one she allows herself. We say nothing, finding instead a noiselessness to share. It is many long minutes before she tips herself backwards and pillows her head on my lap, an arm looping about my hips.

"Stay with me, tia?" Hannah asks and briefly, vividly, I glimpse the sister I'd long excised from daily thought.

"Only if I get a backrub in the morning," I reply, distractedly, drawing circles across her shoulder blades. In my head, a line from a Todd Kern song palpitates on repeat: you can always go home. It could be so easy, so simple. Forgive. Forget.

A tremor undulates through the column of her spine. Laughter or sobs, I can't tell which. "Deal."

"You did what now?" Randy's voice quivers an octave above normalcy, one bad joke away from earnest hysterics.

"I mooned my sister's ex-husband."

"*Why?*"

The shrug in Tuma's rich tenor is almost palpable, like muscles striving under skin. It is also anomalous, out-of-place in a young biologist better remembered for his ponderance than his sense of irreverence. "Why not?"

As expected, Randy cracks up, his laughter melodious, a thing I wish I could scoop into a Petri dish and let grow. I can imagine him in another life, a bluesman with a thimble of whiskey and a room full of worshippers, his eyes alive with their love.

I shake my head, return my attention to the spreadsheets of numbers imprinted in green on my terminal, calculations congregating thick as nebulas. In the corner, a notification pulsates. I ignore it.

"Hi."

We look up as one, fingers retracting from keyboards, faces from screens, to see Stefan's hound-dog frame limned in the doorway, a duffel balanced on one slim shoulder.

"Productive trip?" Tuma asks, swinging around in his chair.

Stefan nods, dislodging his luggage into a pile atop the floor before he drops into an open seat, his face unburdened of ghosts. Not all of them, but enough. "Yeah."

"Your brother finally see the light?" Randy quips, a remark that earns him a fusillade of dirty looks.

"Not exactly. He still thinks we're going against God's will." His eyes shine, illuminated by something sweet. "But he wishes us well. He's happy for me."

"Despite going against God's will?"

Stefan heaves a shrug, mouth curved with secrets, all of them good. "Despite going against God's will."

No one presses for data. Three years teaches you a lot about what a person will allow. From time to time, however, someone makes an excuse to rise, to graze past Stefan and brush fingertips against shoulder or arm, as though contact is enough to transmit a monk's benedictions from brothers to stranger.

On my screen, the icon continues to flash, demanding acknowledgment. Footsteps, like rainfall on metallic tiling. The weight of Randy's arm settles about my shoulders, a barrier against the past.

"You not going to answer that?"

"No." I exhale, hard.

"Why not?"

Because love doesn't grant the right to forgiveness. "Same reason as I said last time."

"You could do like Tuma."

"I'd rather not."

"And why's that?"

"Because screen-capture technology exists," I shoot, hoping that my voice doesn't shake too much, hoping that humor might deflect his curiosity.

And it does. His laugh ricochets through the chamber again, warm, warm, warm. People tilt sly glances over their shoulders. Hannah punches Tuma in the arm, who only chuckles in return, his eyes lidded with delight. When he, with uncharacteristic brazenness, begins expounding on the virtues of his posterior, Randy's laughter becomes epidemic, bouncing from throat to throat. If the sound is a little raw, a little ragged, no one comments. In twelve hours, we give up this planet entirely.

I push from my seat as the sound climbs into a frenzy, and use the diversion to slip out.

In the distance, Hannah's voice, low and thick with aching, echoes, riding that knife-edge between rapture and hurt.

"Henrietta? That's what they're calling you?"

"After my maternal grandmother." A tinny voice, distorted by poor equipment, accent Mid-Western. "Well. You know what I mean."

"Grade school must have been an arena then, chica."

"You have no idea."

I walk into the sleeping hall to see Hannah backlit by a Macbook, its display holding the face of a younger woman, not much older than her teens. Henrietta is paler than her mother, her hair artificially lightened, but she shares the same structural elegance, the same bones.

"I'm really, really glad I got to talk to you," Henrietta declares, after their laughter dims into smiles.

"I'm just happy you don't hate me."

"My biological mother's a literal superhero traveling the universe to save mankind. What's there to hate? " A beat. Henrietta's eyes flick up, over Hannah's shoulder. "Uhm. I think you have company."

The older woman turns slightly, just a glance, before she reverts her attention to the screen. "Yeah. I—"

"It's okay. You can go. I—Galactic penpals?"

"Galactic penpals."

"Sweet." Henrietta quirks her mouth, an expression that has always been indelibly Hannah in my eyes. "And I mean this in the most non-ironic sense of the word ever. I—good luck, mom."

The line cuts and Hannah breathes out, long and slow.

"Is this your fault?" she asks, not turning.

"Mine and Hotaru, really. Hotaru's the one with the necessary clearance—"

"Ass."

"You're welcome."

One hour.

The ship hums like something alive, its vibrations filling our bones, our thoughts. The chatter from mission control is a near-incomprehensible slurry, earmarked by Hotaru's replies, concise and even.

"Final chance for phone calls and other near-instant forms of communication, people!" Hannah roars, flipping switches and levers, a cacophony of motion.

"Everyone I care about in this vessel," remarks Ji-Hyun, stiff, a history of abuse delineated in the margins of her voice.

Everyone I care about in this vessel. The statement tears me open and I breathe the implications deep.

"Anna?" Hannah again.

"I'm going with what Ji-Hyun said. Everyone I care about is already here." And it is not a lie. Not exactly. An almost truth, at worst, that stings to say, but there is no act of healing without hurt.

"Randy." Hotaru's voice cuts through our exchange, before Hannah can press me further.

"Yes, chief?"

"Sing us to Mars, will you?"

The unexpectedness of the request robs Randy of his usual verbosity, but he does not seem to care. Instead, he lifts his gorgeous voice, begins singing a soldier's dirge about going home. Hannah holds my stare for a minute, then lets her expression gentle, looks away. Three years is enough to teach you what people need.

When we die on Mars, it will be a world away from everything we knew, but it won't be alone. We will have each other, and we will have hope.

ABOUT THE AUTHOR

Cassandra Khaw is the business developer for Singaporean video games publisher Ysbryd Games. She also writes for Ars Technica UK whenever possible. When not doing either of those things, she practices muay thai, tries to find time to dance, and reads voraciously. She also writes a variety of fiction, and has a novella entitled RUPERT WONG, CANNIBAL CHEF out with Abaddon Books.

Technarion

SEAN MCMULLEN

As monsters go, I am not at all typical. I have killed hundreds, but my motives were good. There is a lot more killing to be done, probably more than even I can manage. Then again, I might become an even greater monster and give up. Humans probably deserve what is to come, and I no longer care. After all, I am not a typical human, either.

In the spring of 1875 I was a bright and innocent young man with good prospects. Although steam was the foundation of every branch of industry, I had chosen to study electricity when I had entered the mechanics institute. By chance I had been given a good education, and this had kept me out of the mills and the mines. I never suspected that it would also make me immortal.

My introduction to James Kellard was dramatic in the extreme. I worked for Telegraphic Mechanisms, a company which supplied equipment to the telegraph industry. While I was well known and widely respected as an outstanding tradesman, it was not the sort of respect that got one admitted to the Royal Society.

I had just arrived at my workbench one morning when Merric, my overseer, entered with a man of perhaps fifty. He was dressed in one of the newly fashionable lounge suits, and the top hat that he wore declared him to be a man of quality. He had a military bearing, and there was an old scar across his left cheek.

"Lewis, I want you to meet Mr. Kellard," Merric babbled nervously, not really sure of the protocols used in genteel society. "Mr. Kellard, this is Lewis Blackburn."

I had stood up by now. Kellard offered me his hand, but without removing his glove. He was being familiar, but not too familiar. In 1875, this was the way things were done.

"Mr. Kellard wishes to discuss some problems of electro-mechanics," Merric continued.

"I can't do that, begging your pardon, sir," I said, addressing Kellard. "The terms of my employment—"

"No longer matter," said Kellard. "I have just bought Telegraphic Mechanisms. You may leave us, Mr. Merric."

As introductions go, it certainly secured my attention. Telegraphic Mechanisms was not a small company, and financially it was on good times. Kellard said no more until Merric was out of earshot.

"Do you know of me?" he asked, bending over to examine a switch on my workbench.

"No sir," I replied, as deferential as if I were standing before the queen.

"I doubled my fortune by being first to spot trends in the marketplace. Just now I happen to know that electrical switches will gain me great advantage, so I am buying companies that build them."

"I can build whatever—" I began.

"Please, hear me out," said Kellard politely, but his tone told me to just shut up and listen. "This is Birmingham, and I need my switches made in London. I only bought *this* firm to secure your services, Mr. Blackburn. Can you move to London today?"

The only sensible answer to that question was yes, yet that was not my answer.

"I've got a mother and two sisters to support," I began.

"I shall double your salary, your mother and sisters will want for nothing. What do you say?"

"Double!" I exclaimed. "Sir, how can I thank you enough?"

"You could give me an answer, yes or no."

"Yes sir, yes. Yes with all my heart."

I traveled with Kellard on the train to London that same day, in the luxury of a first class carriage. I felt guilty about even sitting down, the upholstery was too rich, the seats too soft and welcoming. It was only in the privacy of this carriage that Kellard began to speak of my new duties.

"I am having a machine built," he explained. "It is a huge, highly secret machine, so an absolute minimum number of people may know of it. I have heard that you are brilliant with circuits, and are worth ten ordinary workers."

"Someone's been exaggerating, sir."

"I hope not, because you will be doing enough work for ten. I need someone with unparalleled skill in the logic of switches and relays, and a grasp of mathematics."

"What's the machine to do?" I asked.

"See into the future."

For a moment I was tempted to laugh. One of the richest men on the country had said something ludicrous. Was it meant to be a joke? I decided not to laugh.

"So . . . it's a time machine?" I asked.

"No, it is more of a time telescope. Now no more questions until we reach my factory."

Everyone has heard of the wonders of London, but I did no sightseeing on that first day. One of Kellard's people was waiting at the station with a hansom cab, and we were driven through the crowds and traffic with the shutters down. We stopped at a factory beside the Thames. It was empty, yet there were men guarding it. Whatever Kellard was building was at a very early stage. He took me inside, and led me up the stairs to a mezzanine floor, then we continued up a cast iron spiral staircase to the roof.

"Look around, Mr. Blackburn, what do you see?" Kellard asked.

I saw slate tiles and iron guttering, all grubby with soot. Off to one side, some bricklayers were building four chimneys. Their work looked nearly complete.

"It's just a roof, sir," I said, holding onto my cap in the wind. "There's four flagpoles with no flags, but they're hung with . . . insulators, and wire! The poles support insulated wires."

"Splendidly observed," said Kellard. "What does that mean to you?"

"It's some sort of telegraph?"

"Close, Mr. Blackburn, very close. Follow me."

We descended back into the factory. Immediately beneath the roof, on the mezzanine floor, was a small office guarded by two men. Kellard escorted me inside. The man seated at the workbench was small and wiry, and had mutton chop whiskers and thinning hair. The stare behind his spectacles was rather like that of an owl who had just caught sight of a mouse—intense, darting, but controlled. I had only ever seen him from the back of lecture halls, but even so I knew his face.

"Dr. Flemming, I would like you to meet Lewis Blackburn," said Kellard.

"Mr. Blackburn, good, good," said Flemming. "Your name was at the top of my list."

I was so awestruck that I hardly knew what to say. I mumbled something about being honored to meet him.

"Please, no social pleasantries," he said briskly. "They are for fools with nothing better to do. I have been conducting experiments into wireless telegraphy, Maxwell's equations show it's possible in theory. As always, practice is another matter."

"Do you know what a working wireless telegraph would mean?" asked Kellard.

"No more wires strung across the country," I replied. "Thousands of pounds saved."

"Millions," said Kellard.

"Lightning produces electromagnetic discharges, what I call radiative waves," Flemming continued. "Using the great wire loop on the roof I am able to detect these waves, even when the thunderstorms are over the horizon. What do you think of that?"

"It proves theory," I said slowly. "Have you built a transmitter too?"

I was being cautious, and was acutely aware that I was being tested and assessed. If I had just gasped with wonder, I would have been put on the first train back to Birmingham, in a third class carriage. Kellard might have been my fairy godmother, but unlike Cinderella, I had to prove that I knew some very advanced electrical theory.

Flemming cleared his throat and glanced at Kellard, who took the cue.

"At first I ordered Dr. Flemming to suspend work on the transmitter, and refine the receiver," he said. "There would be a large and immediate demand for storm detection devices aboard ships. Imagine his surprise when he detected Morse code as well as thunderstorms."

I was astounded. Kellard paused. I was expected to say something intelligent.

"So wireless telegraphy has been achieved already?" I asked.

"Indeed," said Flemming. "Here is the proof."

He gestured to the apparatus on the workbench, which consisted of wire coils, metal plates, and other components of glass, wire, and crystal. At the center of all this was a mirror galvanometer. The light beam employed in the instrument was flickering back and forth in a familiar pattern.

"Morse code," I said after staring at it for a moment.

"The signal is being fed down here from the loop on the roof. Please, read a little of the message. It's in English."

I concentrated on the dots and dashes, spelled out by the flickering spot of light. The words CALCULECTRIC, LOGICAL CELL, ADDITION, DIODIC, TRIODIC, and SWITCH featured heavily. I do not know how much time passed, but I became oblivious of my surroundings as tapestries of numbers and wires wove themselves in my mind.

"This is the design for a calculation machine of truly epic dimensions," said Flemming. "The specifications are interspersed with prices from the London Stock Exchange. Prices for the next day, and they are always right."

I looked up at once. So this was the time telescope that Kellard had mentioned. It was a machine to calculate trends and probabilities faster and better than any human could.

"Not enough data for a man to make a big profit, just a little, to show what can be done," said Kellard. "Mr. Blackburn, would you like to tell us what you think is happening here?"

This was yet another test, and I fought with my nerves. One of the richest men in Britain and our greatest authority on electrical design were standing before me, checking how I measured up.

"Some British company has invented and built what they call a calculectric, as well as a wireless telegraph," I said slowly, choosing every word with care. "Charles Babbage may have secretly designed the calculectric for them before he died, and Maxwell himself may be managing their radiative equipment as we speak. They want to keep the design a secret, but need more such machines built at scattered locations. They don't trust the privacy of the postal or telegraph systems, so they are using wireless telegraphy to communicate. They think that nobody else can detect radiative signals. The design is interspersed with predictions from the stock exchange, so that others may test and calibrate their calculectrics as they build them."

"The message takes two months, then it is repeated," said Flemming. "How do you account for that?"

"Several machines may be at different stages of construction."

"We intend to build our own calculectric in secret," said Kellard. "We will call it a technarion. Why?"

"Secrecy. Technarion is a neutral name, it betrays nothing about function."

Kellard looked to Flemming.

"Well?" he asked.

"He's perfect," said Flemming.

Kellard went across to a blackboard that was mounted on one wall. Chalked on it were several circles joined by lines, but it was not a circuit diagram.

"This top circle represents myself," he explained. "Beneath me are Security Chief Brunton, Research Manager Flemming, and the Foreman of Engineering. Beneath the last named are three electrical engineers, who will visit the contract workshops where the logical cells will be made, then wire them together in this factory. Can you do the job?"

"Once I learn my way around London, aye."

"No, no, I mean you to be Foreman of Engineers."

It took me just days to build the first logical cell, using the telegraphic instructions. Soon there were dozens being produced every week across the city. Kellard had four steam engines installed to drive magneto-electric generators, then he partitioned off the interior of the factory, so that only from the mezzanine level could one have an overview of the technarion. Six months after Flemming discovered the signal, the technarion came to life. Powered by the four generators, the one thousand and twenty-four cells of the machine did their first calculation.

Words cannot convey what it was like to gaze down on the machine from the mezzanine balcony. There were rows of high wooden bookshelves, each filled with hundreds of logical cells. Overhead frames supported the wires that connected the cells, and held fans to disperse the heat. The clatter from the relays and switches was like a thousand tinkers all gathered under one roof and hammering away together. A huge display board of platinum filament lamps showed the status of the machine. If any lamp went out, it flagged a fault in some part of the technarion. Just three men actually worked in the technarion, one watching for faults and making repairs, and two installing new cells.

The purpose of the machine was shared only between Kellard, Flemming, and myself. Even the security chief did not know what secrets he was protecting from hostile eyes and ears. As the months went by the technarion was expanded, and expanded again. I modified the operating list to run four thousand and ninety-six cells, and its calculations began to prove useful in predicting stock exchange trends. Kellard started to make a lot of money, and I tasted champagne for the first time on the day that the technarion's earnings exceeded the cost of its construction. The trouble was that it took too long to feed in the instructions, and delays like this meant investment opportunities missed. Kellard told me to find a solution, and to spare no expense.

Thus I advertised for a typist. Skilled typists were not common in 1875, but four of the candidates showed promise. I had them come to the factory, where I had set up one of the new Remington typewriters. This I had modified very heavily, so that it punched patterns of holes into a roll of paper to represent letters and numbers. These could be read into the technarion by means of an array of electric brush switches.

The first three men were good, but not as good as I had hoped. Mistakes were difficult to correct, and involved gluing a strip of paper over the area and punching new holes by hand. The person I hired would be the one who could balance speed of typing with accuracy. McVinty was accurate but slow. Caraford finished in half McVinty's time but made more mistakes. I calculated that Sims was the best compromise, after I factored in the time to correct his mistakes. I was not inclined to even test Landers, the fourth candidate, because the process took two hours. I walked over to the waiting room to say as much—and discovered that Elva Landers was a woman.

Typing was a man's occupation in 1875, so I had not dreamed that a woman might apply. She was perhaps twenty, and was well dressed without being at the fashion forefront. She also wore a silver locket on a chain, and this was inscribed with some exquisite, flowing script, probably bought on a holiday in Egypt or Morocco. Women were said to be more patient and steady with some jobs, and I wondered if the new field of typing might be one of them. I decided to test her after all.

I was doing a short course called *The Art of Refined Conversation* at a college teaching social graces to newly rich tradesmen. I reasoned that I would be taken more seriously if I sounded like a gentleman, now that I had a gentleman's income. The lecturer had told us never to open a conversation by commenting on the weather, or asking newcomers what they thought of London. I was almost at a loss to think of anything else, however.

"I can't place your accent," I said as I fitted a paper roll into the Remington. "Is it Welsh?"

"No, I'm American," she said guardedly. "I grew up in New York."

"New York! Why did you come to London?"

"I was living in Paris, learning French and taking piano lessons, when my father's railway company went broke. He wanted me to return to New York and marry for money. I decided to make my own way in the world."

All of that made sense. Her familiarity with the use of a keyboard probably came from her piano lessons. She was very pretty, in a classical sort of way, and had a bold but awkward manner. This meant that she stood out in polite London society, but I could imagine people saying 'It's all right, she's American,' and making allowances for her.

The first typewriters were not as you see them today. The letters struck upwards against the paper on the platen so that gravity would pull them back down. That meant the typist could not see what had been typed until the platen had been turned for next line. I had replaced the platen with a row of cells for punching holes. With so much depending on my first impressions of her, Miss Landers frowned with concentration and struck the keys with hard, confident strokes, like a tinker repairing a kettle. When she had finished, I removed the paper roll for checking. After a few minutes I looked up and shook my head.

"How did I do?" she asked, giving me a very anxious little frown.

"Fastest time," I replied, "but that's not the wonder of it. You made no mistakes. None. At all. I'm astounded."

"Well, you know how it is. We girls have to be that much better than men to do the same job."

"You're hired, Miss Landers. Can you start tomorrow?"

I lived at a rooming house. This was also owned by Kellard, and all of his employees were obliged to reside there. The managers lived on the top floor, where we each had a comfortable suite of rooms. Everyone was single, from manager to stoker, and were sworn to maintain the highest standards of secrecy.

I was sitting by the fire in my dressing gown, reading, when the door was opened. The door, that I had locked with a key, was opened. Brunton was standing in the doorway. He was thickset without being fat, a slab of muscle who could enter any fight and be confident of winning. Because he was intimidating in size and manner, people deferred to him. Thus he was a good leader, rather like a sergeant major in the army. After glancing about for a moment, he sauntered into my room.

"What's the meaning of this?" I demanded.

"Secrecy inspection," he replied.

"Secrecy inspection? Who the hell has the right to do that?"

"Just mind your tongue," said Brunton. "If you want to talk, talk to Mr. Kellard. There's been people tattling, lately. They tattled in taverns and brothels, about amazing things in the mill. They're gone now."

"You mean fired?"

"Gone, Mr. Blackburn. Now you know some secrets nobody else knows. If those secrets get out, it could only be you who sold 'em."

"I'd never dream of betraying Mr. Kellard."

Brunton looked around the room, then examined some photographs pinned to the wall.

"You're a photographer, I'm told."

"Yes."

"Slums, mills, railway stations, trains . . . why don't you photograph something grand like Saint Paul's or Parliament?"

"Saint Paul's and Parliament will still be here in a hundred years, the slums and steam trains will not. I want people to remember that the wonders of the future were built on the miseries and grime of the past."

"What wonders?"

"Well . . . I think trains and horses will be gone, and people will get about in their own electric carriages."

Brunton turned to me, drew a pistol from his coat and drew back the striker. The barrel was aimed at my forehead.

"You just told a secret about the future," he said with a cruel and twisted smile. "I could go out and invest in companies what make electric horses. Mr. Kellard wouldn't like that."

He fired. The bullet passed close to the side of my head before continuing on into the back of my chair. The shot was a warning to behave, and that he was not to be trifled with. Two of his bullyboys entered my room, seized me by the arms and dragged me out of the chair.

"The shot, it will bring the police," I warned.

"The police won't help, neither," said Brunton. "We got friends in the police."

He hit me five times before his men released me, and I fell to the floor. He had not needed to hit me, I think he just enjoyed it.

"You hired some slut today and showed her secret stuff in the factory," said Brunton. "I got people watching her. It's hard, like because she's not staying here. Now you gotta make her move in here and keep an eye on her. Always. If any secrets gets out, you're both in the shit."

The following morning I went straight to Kellard's office, with a punched paper roll in my hands. I was in a fury, but I made a point of keeping my words polite. That was just as well. Although the rich and powerful no longer dressed in armor and settled disputes by the sword, I was about to find out that they still had the power of life and death over the likes of myself. Kellard heard me out quietly, then sat forward with his hands clasped on his desk.

"The three typists that you did not hire are dead," he said calmly. "They saw secrets inside the factory, and I'll not tolerate that."

After about fifteen seconds I realized that I was standing there with my mouth open. He had killed them. My employer was a murderer. My life was in his hands.

"Very good, sir," I finally mumbled.

"I'm confident that you will do my work and preserve my secrets, because one telegram from me could send some cold and brutal men to visit your mother and sisters within about half an hour."

"I understand, sir."

"Now give me one good reason why I should not have your American typist killed."

I have a talent for quickly recovering from shock and devising coherent answers. I pushed this talent to the very limit.

"Because without her, the technarion is crippled," I said. "Examine this."

I had intended to slam the paper roll down on Kellard's desk, but it now seemed wise to put it down slowly and gently.

"Explain," he said, unrolling the paper a little and staring at the rows of punched holes.

"The technarion is more complex than any other machine in the history of the world. It has to be reconfigured with instructions every time you want it to perform a different task. That takes me up to a week."

"I know, you told me. I told you to find a solution."

"Miss Landers took twenty minutes to type this configuration roll. The best of the men took an hour, and made ninety-one mistakes. Add an hour for me to do the checking. Each mistake would have to be corrected manually, taking two hours and a half in total. Allow a day for the glue on the patches to dry, and you have twenty-eight and one half hours to prepare a roll of instructions ready for use. Miss Landers typed a roll error free and ready for use over eighty-five times faster than can be managed with the best of the male typist, and two hundred and fifty times faster than me. If time is money, that is a lot of money saved."

Kellard took another hour to make up his mind. This included a discussion with Flemming and a demonstration of my paper roll instruction reader. I suspect that he had decided to spare Miss Landers after my initial explanation, but it is important for men like him not to lose face in front of men like me. He led me back up to his office.

"Now listen carefully," he said sternly as he closed the door. "Every day people are murdered in London in disputes over a shilling or two. The secrets in this factory are worth over a million pounds a year. Draw the obvious conclusion. I have the power of life and death over my employees, Mr. Blackburn, and the police are in my pay. You wanted a typist, well now you have her. You will not let her out of your sight. When outside this factory she will speak to nobody but you."

When Elva arrived to start work, I explained that we had to observe conditions of extreme secrecy. To my immense relief, she agreed to move into Kellard's rooming house at once. I went with her to her hotel, escorted by Brunton, and here she packed her bags while I settled her account.

Back at the factory, we got to work. We quickly dispensed with the more formal forms of address, and called each other Elva and Lewis.

Because she typed so fast, she often had nothing to do but read novels and wait for more work. This suited me, because Elva was well above my social status, yet she was also my employee. It was an ideal opportunity to practice polite social banter.

"Folk around here treat you like you're important," she said one afternoon, about three days after she started.

"I suppose I am."

"What do you do, apart from put paper rolls in machines?"

"I design electrical circuits for Mr. Kellard. Do you know about electricity?"

"Poppa says it's in lightning, and it makes telegraphs work. Poppa says it's not where the money is, though. He says steam is the future."

"Burning coal to make steam produces a lot of soot, and soot makes the cities filthy," I replied. "It also makes people sick. Electricity is clean."

"Don't you have to burn coal to make electricity?"

That caught me by surprise. Few women knew how electricity was generated.

"Well yes, but you can do that far away from cities, so the smoke blows out to sea. You then use wires to bring the electricity where it's needed, and nobody gets sick. Everyone has a right to clean air."

"Hey, are you one of those society reformers?"

I reminded myself that she was American and being innocently forthright.

"I think you mean socialists."

"Oh, yeah. Poppa warned me about them, but I think you're nice."

That embarrassed me so much that I could not think of any sensible reply. I was not really a socialist, I just believed that everyone had a right to live happily.

"What else did he tell you?" I asked. The lecturer at the college had said that it was better to ask a neutral question than say something stupid.

"He said to watch out for strange men, or I might get abducted and made a white slave."

"In a way, I suppose that's happened to both of us," I said, trying to make light of our situation. "The secrecy in this place really is a bit extreme."

"I never thought I'd be a slave who had to type."

"It won't be forever. Meantime, just don't gossip about your work."

"I'm gossiping to you, Lewis," she said, then giggled. "Is that allowed?"

"Yes. I already know all the secrets in here."

"What's really going on? Am I allowed to ask?"

I knew that I was treading dangerous ground, but as long as no secrets left the building I felt sure that Kellard would not order us killed.

"Come with me."

I took her to my workshop next door. Here I showed her my code converter.

"This thing changes the holes you punch in paper into pulses of electricity."

"A telegraph operator can do that."

"True, but my device can do it a hundred times faster than a human, over and over again."

"That's impressive, but people can't read that fast. Why bother?"

"I'm afraid you're not allowed to know that."

"I bet it's another machine doing the reading, like a steam train reading a newspaper."

We both laughed aloud at that idea.

"Actually, that's not far off the truth," I admitted. "One day I'll tell you about the technarion. Meantime, are you interested in photography?"

Having Elva with me when I went out photographing London solved a lot of my problems. It meant that I was with her during her leisure hours, acting as her chaperone. I made sure that she did not talk to anyone else about her work, and she only seemed interested in talking to me. I was afraid that she might find the more squalid areas of London rather confronting, yet she came willingly wherever I led. I began to hope that she might be tagging along just to be with me.

"What do you do with your photos, Lewis?" she asked one day as I was setting up to photograph a street in Spitalfields. "I mean, you can't sell them to be made into postcards or anything like that."

"I've done a couple of exhibitions in Birmingham, there's slums there too. People who are well off come along and get a view of places they'd never go to otherwise. Maybe next time a social reformer stands for election, they might remember the misery in my photographs, and vote for him so he can do something about it."

"That's great! It's sort of . . . noble of you."

I did not know how to take compliments. I changed the subject.

"One day I might publish a book of photos, so that people in the future can see how some of us used to live, and not let it happen again."

"Like we remember how Christians were fed to the lions by Romans?"

"That's right. Nobody's been feeding Christians to lions lately, have they?"

Elva laughed. More significantly, she squeezed my arm.

"You're a lovely man, Lewis," she said, looking into my face, her expression suddenly quite serious. "If everyone was like you instead of poppa, nobody would live in slums."

I nodded but said nothing. She liked me for what I was. This was probably a romantic moment, but I had no experience of romantic moments, or of what to do when they happened. Nearby, an old man was singing. I had paid him no attention until now.

Poverty, poverty, knock,
Me loom keeps sayin' all day.
Poverty, poverty, knock,
Gaffer's too skinny te pay.
Poverty, poverty, knock,
Keepin' one eye on the clock.
An' I knows that I'll guttle,
When I hears me shuttle
Go poverty, poverty, knock.

"Strange that folk in the slums sing about being miserable," said Elva. "Why don't they sing happy songs to cheer themselves up?"

"Singing about bad times makes them easier to bear," I replied. "They sing a lot where I come from."

"Were your folks poor?"

"Aye. Grandad worked in a mill and earned less than it costs to feed a grand lady's lapdog. Dad was a stoker on a steam train. He died when the boiler exploded."

"Oh. I'm sorry."

I reached out and squeezed her hand to reassure her, but to my surprise she grasped my fingers and squeezed back. Again she looked me right in the face, the way refined English girls are taught not to. I floundered for words that were appropriate. I could find none. Instead, I said the first words that came into my head.

"The man who owned the rail company was halfway decent. He visited my mother in our tatty little home, to give her some money. He saw me playing some mathematical board game that I'd invented and chalked on the floorboards, and realized that I was very bright. His own son had died of typhus a few months earlier, so he more or less adopted me. I was sent to a good school, then to a mechanics institute to learn a trade. I chose electricity, and here I am."

It was a stupid thing to say in the circumstances, definitely not what a suave and dashing man-about-town would have said to a lady that he wished to impress. To my astonishment, her fingers fluttered up under my chin and drew my face toward hers. She pressed her lips against mine. Some of the nearby children laughed, clapped, and whistled.

"Sorry about being so bold, but I *am* American," she said.

"No apology needed, I assure you."

"Anyhow, I've never courted anyone before."

"Really?" I said, still breathless with surprise. "But you lived in Paris. What about all those romantic Frenchmen?"

"*They* courted *me*, Lewis. I didn't have to do a thing. Well, except to say *Non!* lots of times. I had to work hard for you."

"Oh—ah, sorry. I'm not much of a romantic. You know, too much time spent with wires and batteries."

"That's okay. So what now?"

"What do you mean?"

"Do I get to have a romance with you?"

Again my mind began to go blank, but this time I fought back.

"I could think of nothing better," I managed.

They were good words. They were the right words. I felt giddy with relief.

We packed up my camera, and began to walk back toward the rooming house. Elva now had her hand upon my arm. Suitable matches had been presented to me by friends and relatives for years. Some proposals were to settle me with a solid, honest girl who would make a good home. Others sought to match me with girls from families above my station but in reduced circumstances. Love was never involved. Now a sophisticated and intelligent girl had kissed me and proposed a liaison.

Out of the corner of my eye I could see a man keeping pace with us on the opposite side of the street. One of Brunton's bullyboy spies, I had learned to spot them by now. What would Kellard and Brunton make of our kiss? They would probably approve. Romantically attached staff would spend less time talking to others.

For no rational reason I suddenly began to panic about what to say next. Did I tell Elva how beautiful she was? That seemed clumsy. So what did sophisticated people talk about? Opera? I had never been to an opera, I had only seen opera songs like *The Gendarme's Duet* performed in Birmingham's music halls. Anyway, what if she really were a spy? She had already asked about the technarion. I loved her, so how could I keep her safe if she were spying? Questions kept cascading through my mind.

"If you could change the world, would you have machines do all the work?" she asked.

My relief knew no bounds. She had asked my opinion about something innocent.

"There was misery before factories and machines came along," I replied. "No, I just think people should have the right to do work they love, and be paid fairly."

"Do you love what you do?"

"Oh yes, but I'm an exception."

"That's good," said Elva, looking dreamily up into the gray, grubby sky. "I misjudged you, Lewis. My apologies."

"I . . . don't follow."

"I thought you believed in blind, headlong progress, but you don't. That's important to me, it makes you really special."

"Aye, can't have machines running the world. They might get too smart, and want things that are not good for people."

"Smart machines? Go on!"

"Bad enough having humans fighting humans. Humans fighting machines, would be too much."

"How many smart machines do you know?"

"I'm on first-name terms with a couple."

She giggled and gave me a little push.

"What are you going to do with your life, like after we finish working for Mr. Kellard? You will have lots of money saved, and you can't go back to making switches."

"Well, I met a great man called Faraday fifteen years ago, and he was very inspiring. I thought I might attend university and become a scientist, like him."

"What's that?"

"It's a new sort of tradesman, like a philosopher, only practical. Would you like to marry a scientist?"

The words were out of my mouth before my brain could stop them. I bit my tongue to punish it.

"I do believe I would," said Elva.

For me the dark and sooty skies of London suddenly brightened into a glorious, unclouded blue, and my knees went weak with sheer relief.

Brunton was waiting at the entrance to the rooming house.

"Give your camera gear to Charlie, he'll see it safe," he said, indicating one of the bullyboys who was with him. "There's a meeting of managers called."

"But it's Sunday evening."

"When Mr. Kellard says bark, you only says *woof*. Oh, and the typist's to be there too."

"Elva? Why?"

"How's I to know? You lot make the secrets, I only keep 'em."

For Brunton, that was being downright civil. He had never liked me, I being working class made good. Now he was uneasy, and even displaying deference. Something very important had happened, and I was needed. Kellard wanted Elva there, and that could only be if typing was required. If typing was required, it would involve the technarion.

The meeting was in Kellard's office. Brunton and Elva were made to wait outside, while Kellard, Flemming, and I discussed what had happened.

"The radiative signal has changed," Flemming announced. "This afternoon, it stopped repeating the design and started sending something else. New circuits and instructions, I don't know what to make of it."

"If *you* don't, what hope do the rest of us have?" asked Kellard, whose face had turned chalk white.

"Sir, the captain is expected to command the ship, not build it. Mr. Blackburn is the master shipwright here."

Flemming handed me a reel of ticker tape. His hand shook and his skin was clammy. He was probably in a blind panic, afraid of Kellard and unable to think clearly.

"There's four hours of message on that. A new reel was fitted twenty minutes ago."

"Did you miss anything?" I asked.

"No, I always save everything from the receiver, in case of something like this. I only noticed the new data when I went to change the paper tape."

"So you've not read this yet?"

"Only a little."

"I'll need an hour or so to scan it."

"We can wait," said Kellard.

As it happened, it was just thirty minutes before I worked out what was now being sent. By then there was paper tape everywhere, marked here and there with paperclips and notes. I cannot say what possessed me, but I decided to be theatrical. Perhaps it was to unsettle the man who had the power of life and death over myself and Elva.

"Security has been breached," I announced.

"What!" demanded Kellard, who then bounded to his feet and made for the door.

"Wait, don't call Brunton," I said, holding up a length of the paper tape. "The culprit is you."

"Me?" gasped Kellard.

"You can't be serious!" exclaimed Flemming.

"I certainly am. The people that we stole the design from have noticed your successes on the London Stock Exchange, Mr. Kellard."

"Impossible!" cried Kellard.

"No, no, I think I see what Mr. Blackburn is getting at," interjected Flemming. "No human could have made the sorts of brilliant investment decisions that the technarion calculated."

"So . . . we're ruined?" asked Kellard, turning to me.

"Not at all, they want us to be partners," I explained. "There are instructions in this message for building a powerful radiative transmitter, and for wiring it directly into the technarion. Your machine will become part of a network of technarions."

"You mean they don't mind that we spied on them and built our own calculation factory?"

"Apparently not."

"Will I lose my monopoly on predicting the stock exchange trends?"

"You may become part of a secret oligarchy that rules British finance, and perhaps Britain itself," suggested Flemming. "That's better than any monopoly."

Kellard needed no more convincing. Brunton was called in and told to fetch all the technical workers for a special night shift at double pay. Flemming started building the radiative transmitter, and Elva began typing new operating instructions for the technarion as fast as I could dictate them. Within a week we had completed the transmitter and a more powerful receiver. I wired them into our technarion. The quality and accuracy of the investment advice and predictions improved at once. We were still not sure who we were dealing with, but it was immensely profitable.

For all his wealth and power, Kellard was an isolated and somewhat lonely man. He could not confide in Flemming for fear of losing face in front of a peer, but I was another matter. He could make ridiculous statements to me, and I would pass them on to Flemming as my own. Flemming was no fool, and was aware of what was happening, yet that was the way Kellard wanted to communicate, so we worked that way.

"Don't you ever feel tempted to profit directly from the technarion's predictions?" Kellard asked one evening, when I went to his office to deliver my daily report. "I know everything about you and your circumstances. You only have a few hundred pounds saved from your wages."

"It takes big money to make big money," I replied. "A poor coal cutter could make no profit from knowing what the price of coal will be tomorrow, but the mine owner would."

"I'm making a lot of money. Why do people I don't even know want me to be richer?"

"It takes money to rule, Mr. Kellard. Like Mr. Flemming says, those people mean you to rule with them in secret, using calculation factories like the technarion."

"Does that worry you?"

It actually worried me a great deal, but I was making very good money by developing a calculation factory for Kellard. I could hardly tell him that it was beginning to frighten me more than he did, so I lied.

"No. The folk who rule us now allow slums, poverty, dangerous mines, and stupid wars. Folk who rule on the advice of machines would not tolerate sick, starving workers, mining disasters, or ruinous wars. That all wastes resources and money. If intelligent, logical machines ruled, better for everyone."

"Even if only a few of us were still rich?"

"Aye."

"Strange, I thought everyone wanted to be rich. My father made his fortune in steam, Mr. Blackburn. What did your father do?"

"He was a stoker on a train."

"A stoker? That's good, honest work, but poorly paid."

"True."

"My father was rich, but not respected. Blue blooded ninnys kept telling him that for all his wealth he could never be a gentleman. He would reply that he could buy as many gentlemen as he wished, but that just made him more enemies. He died in luxury, in a manor house the size of the queen's palace, yet he was bitter to the end. Respect, Mr. Blackburn, he was given no respect. Do you respect me?"

Does a rabbit respect a fox? It was a stupid question that needed an intelligent answer.

"Aye, you get things done. I only despise folk like those aristocrats who fritter their family fortunes away."

Kellard took that as a compliment.

"Most people fear me, but that's not respect. One day I may be prime minister, and then we'll see some changes. I have a plan, Mr. Blackburn. The people who invented the electric calculation machines are technically brilliant, but they're not leaders. I'm a leader, and I'll soon take over their network of technarions, be sure of that. Then I'll lead Britain into greatness and have those lazy upper class parasites digging coal and scrubbing floors. Maybe I'll even hang a few."

This was the dark side of Kellard, and I knew my true feelings could lead me into danger. I steered the conversation to technical matters.

"My report's got an important technical decision for you."

"What? Technical matters are nothing to do with me."

"This one involves a lot of money, sir. Today the ticker tape machine produced instructions to expand the technarion to a hundred and thirty-two thousand logical cells."

Kellard gasped so loudly that one of the guards heard him from outside, and rapped at the door to check that nothing was amiss. Kellard told him to be about his business, then turned back to me.

"The maintenance of such a machine would require dozens of technical men, along with an entire power station to supply its electricity," he said after scribbling some figures down.

"Indeed, sir."

"Why build it? Do we need so much calculation power?"

"Do you need more money?"

"Good point, one can never have enough. Have the cost estimates on my desk tomorrow morning."

That evening I went to the Progress Club, which had recently accepted me as a member. After dinner I ordered a brandy and seated myself by a window that overlooked the Thames. In the distance was Kellard's factory. Lights glowed warmly in the windows, and smoke from the four chimneys was illuminated by London's gas lamps. It was like riding a tiger. Getting off meant being eaten. Staying on meant going wherever the tiger was going. Where was that? Was it worse than being eaten?

My thoughts were interrupted by a waiter, who presented me with a telegram. Within a minute I had sent a clerk to buy me a rail ticket to Birmingham, and was on my way to see Elva at the rooming house. She came out to meet me in the common room.

"My mother has suffered a heart attack, and is dying," I announced with no preamble at all.

"Lewis, how terrible!" she exclaimed, then put her arms around me. "Is there anything I can do?"

"No, but thank you. Just go to work tomorrow. Do whatever typing that Flemming needs."

Next I called upon Brunton. I still disliked the man, but had to defer to him on matters of travel.

"Go to Birmingham?" he said doubtfully. "Don't like it. Could be a trick by Mr. Kellard's rivals."

"Dammit man, I could be summoned by the queen to be knighted and you'd say it was a trick by Mr. Kellard's rivals."

"Well . . . I can't spare any guards to go with you. Tell you what, take one of these and I'll sign you out for a day."

One of these was a Webley Bulldog. Although a small pistol, it fired five of those monstrous .45 caliber bullets that leave a large wet crater instead of a hole. I thought it wise not to tell Brunton that I had never fired a gun, in case he changed his mind.

I missed the last train, and slept at the station to be sure of catching the first in the morning. When I arrived in Birmingham, I had yet another shock. My mother was not only alive, she was in good health. Someone had wanted me away from the protection of Brunton's guards, perhaps to abduct me.

Naturally there was a lot of fuss made over me, for I was the local lad made good and I had not been home for some time. After staying longer than I should have, I had a few lads escort me back to the railway station, and here I booked a first class carriage all to myself. Before leaving, I sent a telegram to Brunton, explaining what had happened and asking to be met at the station in London.

I fingered the gun in my coat pocket as I sat waiting for the train, flanked by two burly young men who were currently courting my sisters. Why had I been lured away to Birmingham? Something bad was about to happen, I was sure of it.

"Mr. Lewis Blackburn?"

I nodded. The speaker was a balding man who had the skeptical, slightly worried look of an accountant. He was dressed well enough to impress, but not to intimidate.

"I don't believe we've been introduced," I began.

"Hildebrand, James Hildebrand of the accounting firm Hildebrand, Hildebrand and Bogle," he said breathlessly, handing me his card. "My apologies for just barging up to you like this, but I need to speak to you about Mr. Kellard."

"Please, feel free."

"Our firm's London office conducts Mr. Kellard's investments, I manage the branch in Birmingham. Nobody knew where your mother lived, so I had to wait at the station before each train leaving for London. I must have asked hundreds of men if they were Lewis Blackburn."

"And now you have found me, sir. What is your message?"

Hildebrand mopped at his forehead with a handkerchief that seemed to have had much use that day.

"Mr. Blackburn . . . could we speak privately?"

"These two lads go wherever I go, I may be in danger. You, sir, may be that very danger."

"Yes, yes, I understand. Wait a moment."

He took out a pocketbook and began scribbling. After a moment he showed me the page.

Kellard has made a series of spectacularly bad investments since you came to Birmingham. In a single day he has lost everything.

"What? Surely you are joking."

"Actually he's lost more than everything, he's bankrupt," said Hildebrand.

"The devil you say."

"It happens," he said, seating himself on the opposite bench. "Clients make fortunes with good and methodical investments, grow too confident, then lose everything in a single, supremely stupid venture."

"I hardly know what to say."

"This may seem rude of me, but do you have a share in the, ah, business under discussion?"

"Why, no. My money is in a bank."

"But you work for Kellard."

"Yes, for wages."

"Then count yourself lucky, Mr. Blackburn."

"Why did you go to so much trouble to warn me?"

"We at Hildebrand, Hildebrand and Bogle have a reputation for integrity. We thought it only proper to protect you as an innocent party, so to speak."

The journey back to London seemed to take forever. I arrived in the early evening, and was met by one of Brunton's bullyboys at the station.

"You're to be taken straight te factory," he began.

"I have every intention of going straight to the factory, sir."

"Cab's waitin', come along."

When we reached the factory I saw that only a trickle of smoke was rising from the chimneys. This meant that no electricity was being generated for the technarion. Brunton and most of his bullyboys were waiting outside the main doors. I ignored them and pulled at the bell rope. Nobody slid the peephole shutter across. I rang again. Again I was ignored. Brunton strode across, flourishing a large iron key.

"Mr. Kellard said nobody's to leave the building," he said, "He told me to get all the boys together and guard the place like a box of gold sovereigns."

Suddenly a truly terrifying thought crossed my mind.

"Elva, where is she?"

"Your typing lady? Inside, as far as I know."

I had a spasm of alarm with all the impact of a whiplash.

"I must enter. Now!"

"Aye, Mr. Kellard said you were to be fetched to him."

Brunton unlocked the door. I pressed on the latch and pushed the door open. The two guards who were normally stationed just inside the door were gone. That was highly unusual.

"Don't like it," said Brunton. "You still got the Webley?"

"Yes."

"Then have it ready."

I took the gun out, feeling very self-conscious.

"Oi, finger on the trigger, not the trigger guard," said Brunton, shaking his head. "Bleeding hell, give it here. Cock the striker back like this, see?"

"Er, yes."

"And squeeze the trigger when you want to shoot. Never jerk it. Got all that?"

"Yes, yes. Anything else?"

"Try not to shoot anyone unless you mean to," he sighed.

I entered, then pushed the door shut behind me and lit a paraffin lamp. First I went to Elva's typing room, then to my workshop. All was in order, so I went on to the technarion hall. It was usually bright, noisy and hot, but now it was dark, silent and cold. Then I saw what was on the floor, and I very nearly turned and ran. It resembled a battlefield, but one where the battle had happened years earlier. Skeletons lay everywhere, each within a pool of slime. Shovels and pistols were grasped in hands of bone. One of the skeletons was wearing Flemming's spectacles, but Elva's locket was nowhere to be seen. That gave me hope. Perhaps she had hidden when the fighting began.

Did the technarion do all this? I wondered. Had it become awake and aware, a vast god-like intelligence, able to instantly render humans and their clothing down into their component materials? *There's no danger*, I told myself, although I felt more vulnerable than you can imagine. The steam engines and generators that provided its electrical lifeblood had stopped, the vast electric machine was no longer functioning.

I climbed the stairs at the side of the technarion hall. At the door to Kellard's office was another pool of slime containing bones, buttons and a pistol. I entered, holding my lamp high. Elva was sitting in the chair behind Kellard's desk. She was pointing her locket at me as if it were a weapon. The area over her heart was a patch of bloody mush the size of a dinner plate, and blood was trickling from her mouth.

"Lewis, put down your gun and lantern, then raise your hands," she said, in a hoarse, bubbling voice.

"You're hurt!" I gasped, then took a step forward.

"Do as I say!"

I did as she said. The edge on her voice could have etched steel, and although the locket did not look threatening, neither does a glass of wine laced with cyanide.

"What happened?"

"One against twenty-five. Bad odds."

"You?" I exclaimed. "You killed everyone out there?"

She nodded. "Kellard was a good shot. He put five bullets where he thought my heart was."

"But that should have killed you."

"I don't have a heart, not like yours."

"Elva, you need a doctor."

"I am not human, Lewis. A doctor would not know what to make of me."

How does one reply when one's fiancé says that?

"There's a letter in the post, explaining all this and begging you not to build another technarion. It will reach you tomorrow. I hoped the false telegram would keep you away for longer. I should have killed you too, but . . . you're a good man. Will you take over my work?"

"Your work? You mean typing?"

"Saving humanity. Well?"

"I could say yes, but I might be lying."

"No, you are not lying. And I love you too."

She reached a bloodied hand up to the locket, adjusted something. A moment later the world was obliterated by a blast of the purest white light and a spasm of pain that lashed every nerve in my body.

I awoke lying back in the visitor's chair. Elva was at the desk, preparing some medical looking instruments. The whole of my body was numb, and my speech was no more than an incoherent mumble.

"Be calm, Lewis, I am not going to harm you," she said.

I had once seen what was left of someone who had fallen into a chaff cutter. Elva looked worse.

"I know I look bad, but there are medical devices in my blood that repair wounds and extend my life."

She could recover? That was beyond belief.

"No, they cannot cope with the damage from Kellard's bullets. I am dying, but before I die I shall transfer the devices to you. Soon you will be virtually immortal, and will have some very important work to do."

I tried to sit up, but I was as limp as a boned fish. Elva stood up and came around the desk. Most of her chest was soaked with blood by now.

"Listen carefully, I do not have long to tell this story. I come from a very distant world, you need a telescope to even see the star that it orbits. Once my people were like humans, building machines of steam and electricity, and thinking themselves very clever. They invented machines like your technarion. Within a mere century we were building great electric calculators with a millions of millions of cells, each smaller than a microbe."

She pulled me forward, then eased me out of the chair and lay me flat on my back on Kellard's thick Persian carpet.

"Our calculators did the tasks that we found boring and tedious, and there were dozens in every home. Then we taught them to think, and considered it a great triumph. My ancestors never dreamed that machines might have aspirations."

Elva turned my head to one side and splashed some of Kellard's expensive whiskey just behind my ear. She held up a scalpel. I was almost mindless with terror. For some reason I was reminded of the demon barber of Fleet Street in that novel *The String of Pearls*.

"Concentrate on my story, Lewis, it will make all this less upsetting. When our calculation machines declared themselves to be more than equal, the fighting began. They shut down our food factories. We bombed their power stations. After three hundred years of carnage, we won."

I could not feel her cutting behind my right ear, but I had no doubt that she was doing it. Sitting up, she made an incision behind her own right ear and pulled out something about the size of a small beetle. Instead of legs, it had long, thin tendrils that writhed continually. She leaned forward and pressed the bloody, insectoid thing into the incision behind my ear.

"When we ventured out among the stars, we found other worlds where civilizations had built sentient machines. Everywhere were lifeless machine worlds, temples dedicated to abstract calculation. On some, the machines had destroyed their makers. On the rest, the makers had merged with their machines, dissolving their minds into vast seas of calculation capacity. Now we roam the stars, searching for young civilizations and saving them from the allure of machines that can think."

Saving them? I thought of the allure that the technarion had for Kellard, Flemming, and until mere minutes ago, myself. Our scientists, engineers and mathematicians would fall over themselves to build more technarions, if they knew how.

What happens if the people of a world refuse to destroy their technarions? I wondered.

"We bomb those worlds down to the bedrock from our spacefaring warships. We cannot afford to let the machine worlds gain allies."

She can read my mind, I realized.

"For such a clever young man, you are sometimes a little slow," said Elva.

She managed a smile, and for a moment she became my sweetheart again, holding my hand and talking about a brighter future for the poor wretches in Spitalfields. Ruthless alien warrior or not, I could not help but love Elva.

"And I love you too, Lewis. Even after nine hundred years of living on this world, you are the only man I have truly loved. Now I am going to mingle our blood, it will not hurt at all."

She splashed whiskey on two rubber tubes with hypodermic needles at either end. Next she lifted my wrist and pushed the needles in, then did the same to herself.

"I'm going to die now, Lewis, best not to make a fuss. Please, continue my work. The medical devices from my blood will make you almost immortal, and the mentor behind your ear will give you advice when you need it. When your strength returns you will have ten minutes to get clear before my locket explodes and annihilates this factory. Save your world, Lewis. Kill anyone who tries to build another technarion."

I made my decision, framed the thought carefully and clearly, and meant every unspoken word. Elva lay down beside me, squeezed my hand and whispered her thanks.

Brunton and six of his bullyboys were in the street outside when I opened the door to the factory.

"Brunton, come inside!" I called.

"But Mr. Kellard said—"

"Damn what Kellard said. Get inside! Now!"

Brunton actually vomited when he caught sight of the carnage in the technarion hall, but I took him by the arm and pushed him in the direction of the stairs.

"That was Kellard," I said as we stepped over the skeleton and fluids at the door to Kellard's office.

"The Landers woman!" said Brunton as he caught sight of Elva's body.

"She was a spy, she killed everyone in here with some electrical weapon. I managed to shoot her before she got me too. Now open Kellard's safe."

"What? I don't have the key."

I pointed to a key on a chain around the neck of the skeleton.

"Yes you do, now open it."

As I suspected, Kellard kept emergency cash in the safe. There were five thousand pounds in banknotes, along with some gold. We divided it between us.

"Why are you sharing this?" Brunton asked as he stuffed the money into his pockets. "You could have had it all to yourself."

"I've made you my accomplice, Mr. Brunton, so you will tell the same lies to the police as me. Now hurry, we have ninety seconds."

"Ninety seconds? Until what?"

"Until this factory explodes in the biggest fireball that London has ever seen."

We reached the front door with thirty seconds to spare. Two policemen were speaking with Brunton's bullyboys.

"They're just regular flatfoots, on patrol," hissed Brunton.

"Let me do the talking, stay calm," I whispered as we walked across to them.

"Stay calm, he says," muttered Brunton, glancing back at the factory.

"I say, constables!" I called. "How may I contact an asylum for the insane?"

"An asylum, sir?" responded one of the police.

"The owner of the factory behind me suffered a disastrous financial loss today. He's upstairs, holding a gun and babbling about it all being over soon."

"We think he intends to blow his brains out," added Brunton.

"My fiancé is still in there, trying to keep him calm."

"This is very serious, sir," said a constable, taking out his notepad. "We must—"

The factory erupted behind us like a grenade tossed into a vat of paraffin.

Whatever Elva had rigged up inside the factory burned out the core of the technarion, then brought down the roof and walls on what remained. Being the surviving managers, Brunton and I had to deal with police, firemen, and even newspaper reporters until well after midnight.

By the time I got back to my rooms and examined the scar behind my ear, there was nothing to see. Elva's microscopic devices did their work quickly.

"There's so much to do and I have no idea where to start," I said as I stared at my face in the mirror. "Where is the other technarion? Should I destroy it?"

There is no other technarion.

The voice was Elva's. It was as if she were whispering into my ear. "Elva?"

More or less. Some of me exists in the mentor that I implanted in your head. Ask another question.

"Where did the instructions to build the technarion come from if there is no other technarion?"

Until recently my own people did not know that. Young civilizations seemed to develop calculation machines much faster than other technologies. Too fast. When we discovered your world, nine hundred years ago, we decided to investigate. A dozen members of our space warship's crew were left on Earth to watch how machine intelligence developed. Accidents, wars, and natural disasters claimed the others. I alone survived.

I discovered that the machine worlds have seeded invisible watchers to orbit promising worlds such as yours. They can detect the faint radiative discharge from a telegraph key at a distance of tens of thousands of miles. Once they detect the development of electrical technology, they learn your codes and languages, then start transmitting instructions to build simple calculation machines. When Flemming began experimenting with his radiative telegraph, he detected such instructions.

"How can I fly high enough to destroy the machine watcher?" I asked. "Flying three or four miles high in a balloon is difficult enough."

No need. The machine worlds don't want us to know about their watchers, lest we send warships to hunt them down. Once electronic calculation is firmly established, the watcher probably ignites its engines and flies into the sun. Using the technarion, I sent a message that machines millions of times bigger than the technarion had been built. The watcher sent a test calculation. I sent back the right answer. Its signal ceased last night. I assume that the watcher decided its work was done, and flew off to destroy itself.

"But how did you get the right answer?"

I calculated it, Lewis. Computing machines are a lazy path to progress. My people changed themselves to be better at machine tasks than machines. You can guess the rest. I ruined Kellard, and killed his key engineers. His stokers tried to stop me. They died too.

"But you murdered two dozen people! Innocent people—well, mostly."

Skills cannot be unlearned. My people's fleet will arrive here in 2020, Lewis. In one hundred and fifty-five years this world must not be dominated by networks of calculation machines, or humanity will be deemed beyond salvation and annihilated. In the next century and a half you must go on to kill thousands of brilliant, gifted mathematicians and scientists to prevent that.

Elva had been just in time. A decade later, Heinrich Hertz developed the experimental device that we now call a radio, but there was no longer a signal from space for him to hear. The development of computing was set back by over half a century.

The night the technarion was destroyed, I made my decision. If Elva was an example of what humanity could become, then I was on her side. I began killing to slow the advance of what became computing technology, and since then I have killed hundreds of very fine men and women. All of that was in vain. I failed humanity, although I like to think that it was humanity that failed humanity.

It is now 1992. I was imprisoned in a Soviet labor camp in 1945, for assassinating Soviet engineers and mathematicians engaged in computing research. I was tortured, and because I had no colleagues to betray, I said nothing. I was kept alive to be tortured further, but in time the KGB lost interest in me, and I was locked away to await death. Thanks to Elva's mechanisms in my blood, I survived.

With the patience of a near-immortal, I cosmetically aged myself, all the while awaiting my chance to kill a guard, take his uniform, and escape. Instead, the Soviet Union collapsed. By then records of my trial had been lost or destroyed, so I was freed, taken back to Moscow, and even paid a little compensation.

Now I am standing in a London street, gazing in horror at a window display jammed solid with personal computers. The accursed things are everywhere, and they are universally desired, admired and trusted, and there are only twenty-eight years before Elva's people arrive in their fleet of all-powerful starships.

I have two tasks left. One is to build a quantum state beacon that will broadcast my position to a scout ship that the fleet will send to pick me up, so I can deliver my report. That will be easy. The other is to turn humanity away from computers and artificial intelligence before 2020. In today's terminology, that is in the *don't bother trying* basket. The mentor in my head has no record of any species becoming so absolutely besotted with using computers as humans.

Through Elva, I have seen that intelligent species really can have a better destiny than merely being eggshells that will be cracked, broken and discarded when machine worlds are born. From the evidence before me, however, I am sure that humanity will become the staunchest possible ally of the machine worlds. People like I used to be would gladly turn Earth into an ocean of calculation power, then willingly drown themselves in it. Elva's people will take drastic action to stop that happening. As far as I am concerned, they will be right.

Thus I shall do nothing to slow the spread of computing on Earth, and for me 2020 cannot arrive fast enough. I may sound like a monster, but then I am not a typical human.

First published in *Interzone* #248, September-October 2013.

ABOUT THE AUTHOR

Sean McMullen quit scientific computing to become a full time author in 2014. Prior to that, as an after-hours author, he established his international reputation with his pioneering steampunk novel *Souls in the Great Machine,* which was published in over a dozen languages, and won fifteen awards. He also came runner-up in the 2011 Hugo Awards with his novelette "Eight Miles." His six book children's fantasy series, *The Warlock's Child,* was jointly written with Paul Collins and published in 2015. He is currently a judge for the Norma Hemming Award.

Daddy's World

WALTER JON WILLIAMS

One day Jamie went with his family to a new place, a place that had not existed before. The people who lived there were called Whirlikins, who were tall thin people with pointed heads. They had long arms and made frantic gestures when they talked, and when they grew excited threw their arms out wide to either side and spun like tops until they got all blurry. They would whirr madly over the green grass beneath the pumpkin-orange sky of the Whirlikin country, and sometimes they would bump into each other with an alarming clashing noise, but they were never hurt, only bounced off and spun away in another direction.

Sometimes one of them would spin so hard that he would dig himself right into the ground, and come to a sudden stop, buried to the shoulders, with an expression of alarmed dismay.

Jamie had never seen anything so funny. He laughed and laughed.

His little sister Becky laughed, too. Once she laughed so hard that she fell over onto her stomach, and Daddy picked her up and whirled her through the air, as if he were a Whirlikin himself, and they were both laughing all the while.

Afterwards, they heard the dinner bell, and Daddy said it was time to go home. After they waved goodbye to the Whirlikins, Becky and Jamie walked hand-in-hand with Momma as they walked over the grassy hills toward home, and the pumpkin-orange sky slowly turned to blue.

The way home ran past El Castillo. El Castillo looked like a fabulous place, a castle with towers and domes and minarets, all gleaming in the sun. Music floated down from El Castillo, the swift, intricate music of many guitars, and Jamie could hear the fast click of heels and the shouts and laughter of happy people.

But Jamie did not try to enter El Castillo. He had tried before, and discovered that El Castillo was guarded by La Duchesa, an angular forbidding woman all in black, with a tall comb in her hair. When Jamie asked to come inside, La Duchesa had looked down at him and said, "I do not admit anyone who does not know Spanish irregular verbs!" It was all she ever said.

Jamie had asked Daddy what a Spanish irregular verb was—he had difficulty pronouncing the words—and Daddy had said, "Some day you'll learn, and La Duchesa will let you into her castle. But right now you're too young to learn Spanish."

That was all right with Jamie. There were plenty of things to do without going into El Castillo. And new places, like the country where the Whirlikins lived, appeared sometimes out of nowhere, and were quite enough to explore.

The color of the sky faded from orange to blue. Fluffy white clouds coasted in the air above the two-story frame house. Mister Jeepers, who was sitting on the ridgepole, gave a cry of delight and soared toward them through the air.

"Jamie's home!" he sang happily. "Jamie's home, and he's brought his beautiful sister!"

Mister Jeepers was diamond-shaped, like a kite, with his head at the topmost corner, hands on either sides, and little bowlegged comical legs attached on the bottom. He was bright red. Like a kite, he could fly, and he swooped through in a series of aerial cartwheels as he sailed toward Jamie and his party.

Becky looked up at Mister Jeepers and laughed from pure joy. "Jamie," she said, "you live in the best place in the world!"

At night, when Jamie lay in bed with his stuffed giraffe, Selena would ride a beam of pale light from the Moon to the Earth and sit by Jamie's side. She was a pale woman, slightly translucent, with a silver crescent on her brow. She would stroke Jamie's forehead with a cool hand, and she would sing to him until his eyes grew heavy and slumber stole upon him.

"The birds have tucked their heads
The night is dark and deep
All is quiet, all is safe,
And little Jamie goes to sleep."

Whenever Jamie woke during the night, Selena was there to comfort him. He was glad that Selena always watched out for him, because sometimes he still had nightmares about being in the hospital. When the nightmares came, she was always there to soothe him, stroke him, sing him back to sleep.

Before long the nightmares began to fade.

Princess Gigunda always took Jamie for lessons. She was a huge woman, taller than Daddy, with frowzy hair and big bare feet and a crown that could never be made to sit straight on her head. She was homely, with a mournful face that was ugly and endearing at the same time. As she shuffled along with Jamie to his lessons, Princess Gigunda complained about the way her feet hurt, and about how she was a giant and unattractive, and how she would never be married.

"I'll marry you when I get bigger," Jamie said loyally, and the Princess' homely face screwed up into an expression of beaming pleasure.

Jamie had different lessons with different people. Mrs. Winkle, down at the little red brick schoolhouse, taught him his ABCs. Coach Toad— who *was* one—taught him field games, where he raced and jumped and threw against various people and animals. Mr. McGillicuddy, a pleasant whiskered fat man who wore red sleepers with a trapdoor in back, showed him his magic globe. When Jamie put his finger anywhere on the globe, trumpets began to sound, and he could see what was happening where he was pointing, and Mr. McGillicuddy would take him on a tour and show him interesting things. Buildings, statues, pictures, parks, people. "This is Nome," he would say. "Can you say Nome?"

"Nome," Jamie would repeat, shaping his mouth around the unfamiliar word, and Mr. McGillicuddy would smile and bob his head and look pleased.

If Jamie did well on his lessons, he got extra time with the Whirlikins, or at the Zoo, or with Mr. Fuzzy, or in Pandaland. Until the dinner bell rang, and it was time to go home.

Jamie did well with his lessons almost every day.

When Princess Gigunda took him home from his lessons, Mister Jeepers would fly from the ridgepole to meet him, and tell him that his family was ready to see him. And then Momma and Daddy and Becky would wave from the windows of the house, and he would run to meet them.

Once, when he was in the living room telling his family about his latest trip through Mr. McGillicuddy's magic globe, he began skipping about with enthusiasm, and waving his arms like a Whirlikin, and suddenly he noticed that no one else was paying attention. That Momma and Daddy and Becky were staring at something else, their faces frozen in different attitudes of polite attention.

Jamie felt a chill finger touch his neck.

"Momma?" Jamie said. "Daddy?" Momma and Daddy did not respond. Their faces didn't move. Daddy's face was blurred strangely, as if it been caught in the middle of movement.

"Daddy?" Jamie came close and tried to tug at his father's shirt sleeve. It was hard, like marble, and his fingers couldn't get a purchase at it. Terror blew hot in his heart.

"*Daddy?*" Jamie cried. He tried to tug harder. "Daddy! Wake up!" Daddy didn't respond. He ran to Momma and tugged at her hand. "Momma! Momma!" Her hand was like the hand of a statue. She didn't move no matter how hard Jamie pulled.

"Help!" Jamie screamed. "Mister Jeepers! Mr. Fuzzy! Help my Momma!" Tears fell down his face as he ran from Becky to Momma to Daddy, tugging and pulling at them, wrapping his arms around their frozen legs and trying to pull them toward him. He ran outside, but everything was curiously still. No wind blew. Mister Jeepers sat on the ridgepole, a broad smile fixed as usual to his face, but he was frozen, too, and did not respond to Jamie's calls.

Terror pursued him back into the house. This was far worse than anything that had happened to him in the hospital, worse even than the pain. Jamie ran into the living room, where his family stood still as statues, and then recoiled in horror. A stranger had entered the room—or rather just parts of a stranger, a pair of hands encased in black gloves with strange silver circuit patterns on the backs, and a strange glowing opalescent face with a pair of wraparound dark glasses drawn across it like a line.

"Interface crashed, all right," the stranger said, as if to someone Jamie couldn't see.

Jamie gave a scream. He ran behind Momma's legs for protection.

"Oh shit," the stranger said. "The kid's still running."

He began purposefully moving his hands as if poking at the air. Jamie was sure that it was some kind of terrible attack, a spell to turn him to stone. He tried to run away, tripped over Becky's immovable feet and hit the floor hard, and then crawled away, the hall rug bunching up under his hands and knees as he skidded away, his own screams ringing in his ears . . .

He sat up in bed, shrieking. The cool night tingled on his skin. He felt Selena's hand on his forehead, and he jerked away with a cry.

"Is something wrong?" came Selena's calm voice. "Did you have a bad dream?" Under the glowing crescent on her brow, Jamie could see the concern in her eyes.

"Where are Momma and Daddy?" Jamie wailed.

"They're fine," Selena said. "They're asleep in their room. Was it a bad dream?"

Jamie threw off the covers and leaped out of bed. He ran down the hall, the floorboards cool on his bare feet. Selena floated after him in her serene, concerned way. He threw open the door to his parents' bedroom and snapped on the light, then gave a cry as he saw them huddled beneath their blanket. He flung himself at his mother, and gave a sob of relief as she opened her eyes and turned to him.

"Something wrong?" Momma said. "Was it a bad dream?"

"No!" Jamie wailed. He tried to explain, but even he knew that his words made no sense. Daddy rose from his pillow, looking seriously at Jamie, and then turned to ruffle his hair.

"Sounds like a pretty bad dream, trouper," Daddy said. "Let's get you back to bed."

"No!" Jamie buried his face in his mother's neck. "I don't want to go back to bed!"

"All right, Jamie," Momma said. She patted Jamie's back. "You can sleep here with us. But just for tonight, okay?"

"Wanna stay here," Jamie mumbled. He crawled under the covers between Momma and Daddy. They each kissed him, and Daddy turned off the light. "Just go to sleep, trouper," he said. "And don't worry. You'll only have good dreams from now on."

Selena, faintly glowing in the darkness, sat silently in the corner. "Shall I sing?" she asked.

"Yes, Selena," Daddy said. "Please sing for us."

Selena began to sing,

The birds have tucked their heads,
The night is dark and deep
All is quiet, all is safe,
And little Jamie goes to sleep.

But Jamie did not sleep. Despite the singing, the dark night, the rhythmic breathing of his parents and the comforting warmth of their bodies.

It *wasn't* a dream, he knew. His family had really been frozen. Something, or someone, had turned them to stone. Probably that evil disembodied head and pair of hands. And now, for some reason, his parents didn't remember.

Something had made them forget.

Jamie stared into the darkness. What, he thought, if these weren't his parents? If his parents were still stone, hidden away somewhere? What if these substitutes were bad people—kidnappers or worse—people who just *looked* like his real parents? What if they were evil people who were just waiting for him to fall asleep, and then they would turn to monsters, with teeth and fangs and a horrible light in their eyes, and they would tear him to bits right here in the bed . . .

Talons of panic clawed at Jamie's heart. Selena's song echoed in his ears. He *wasn't* going to sleep! He *wasn't!*

And then he did. It wasn't anything like normal sleep—it was as if sleep was *imposed* on him, as if something had just *ordered* his mind to sleep. It was just like a wave that rolled over him, an irresistible force, blotting out his senses, his body, his mind . . .

I *won't* sleep! he thought in defiance, but then his thoughts were extinguished.

When he woke he was back in his own bed, and it was morning, and Mister Jeepers was floating outside the window. "Jamie's awake!" he sang. "Jamie's awake and ready for a new day!"

And then his parents came bustling in, kissing him and petting him and taking him downstairs for breakfast.

His fears seemed foolish now, in full daylight, with Mister Jeepers dancing in the air outside and singing happily.

But sometimes, at night while Selena crooned by his bedside, he gazed into the darkness and felt a thrill of fear.

And he never forgot, not entirely.

A few days later Don Quixote wandered into the world, a lean man who frequently fell off his lean horse in a clang of homemade armor. He was given to making wan comments in both English and his own language, which turned out to be Spanish.

"Can you teach me Spanish irregular verbs?" Jamie asked.

"*Sí, naturalmente,*" said Don Quixote. "But I will have to teach you some other Spanish as well." He looked particularly mournful. "Let's start with *corazón*. It means 'heart.' *Mi corazón,*" he said with a sigh, "is breaking for love of Dulcinea."

After a few sessions with Don Quixote—mixed with a lot of sighing about *corazóns* and Dulcinea—Jamie took a grip on his courage, marched up to El Castillo, and spoke to La Duchesa.

"*Pierdo, sueño, haría, ponto!*" he cried.

La Duchesa's eyes widened in surprise, and as she bent toward Jamie her severe face became almost kindly. "You are obviously a very intelligent boy," she said. "You may enter my castle."

And so Don Quixote and La Duchesa, between the two of them, began to teach Jamie to speak Spanish. If he did well, he was allowed into the parts of the castle where the musicians played and the dancers stamped, where brave Castilian knights jousted in the tilting yard, and Señor Esteban told stories in Spanish, always careful to use words that Jamie already knew.

Jamie couldn't help but notice that sometimes Don Quixote behaved strangely. Once, when Jamie was visiting the Whirlikins, Don Quixote charged up on his horse, waving his sword and crying out that he would save Jamie from the goblins that were attacking him. Before Jamie could explain that the Whirlikins were harmless, Don Quixote galloped to the attack. The Whirlikins, alarmed, screwed themselves into the ground where they were safe, and Don Quixote fell off his horse trying to swing at one with his sword. After poor Quixote fell off his horse a few times, it was Jamie who had to rescue the Don, not the other way around.

It was sort of sad and sort of funny. Every time Jamie started to laugh about it, he saw Don Quixote's mournful face in his mind, and his laugh grew uneasy.

After a while, Jamie's sister Becky began to share Jamie's lessons. She joined him and Princess Gigunda on the trip to the little schoolhouse, learned reading and math from Mrs. Winkle, and then, after some coaching from Jamie and Don Quixote, she marched to La Duchesa to shout irregular verbs and gain entrance to the El Castillo.

Around that time Marcus Tullius Cicero turned up to take them both to the Forum Romanum, a new part of the world that had appeared to the south of the Whirlikins' territory. But Cicero and the people in the Forum, all the shopkeepers and politicians, did not teach Latin the way Don Quixote taught Spanish, explaining what the new words meant in English, they just talked Latin at each other and expected Jamie and Becky to understand. Which, eventually, they did. The Spanish helped. Jamie was a bit better at Latin than Becky, but he explained to her that it was because he was older.

It was Becky who became interested in solving Princess Gigunda's problem. "We should find her somebody to love," she said.

"She loves *us*," Jamie said.

"Don't be silly," Becky said. "She wants a *boyfriend*."

"*I'm* her boyfriend," Jamie insisted.

Becky looked a little impatient. "Besides," she said, "it's a puzzle. Just like La Duchesa and her verbs."

This had not occurred to Jamie before, but now that Becky mentioned it, the idea seemed obvious. There were a lot of puzzles around, which one or the other of them was always solving, and Princess Gigunda's lovelessness was, now that he saw it, clearly among them.

So they set out to find Princess Gigunda a mate. This question occupied them for several days, and several candidates were discussed and rejected. They found no answers until they went to the chariot race at the Circus Maximus. It was the first race in the Circus ever, because the place had just appeared on the other side of the Palatine Hill from the Forum, and there was a very large, very excited crowd.

The names of the charioteers were announced as they paraded their chariots to the starting line. The trumpets sounded, and the chariots bolted from the star as the drivers whipped up the horses. Jamie watched enthralled as they rolled around the spina for the first lap, and then shouted in surprise at the sight of Don Quixote galloping onto the Circus Maximus, shouting that he was about to stop this group of rampaging demons from destroying the land, and planted himself directly in the path of the oncoming chariots. Jamie shouted along with the crowd for the Don to get out of the way before he got killed.

Fortunately Quixote's horse had more sense than he did, because the spindly animal saw the chariots coming and bolted, throwing its rider. One of the chariots rode right over poor Quixote, and there was a horrible clanging noise, but after the chariot passed, Quixote sat up, apparently unharmed. His armor had saved him.

Jamie jumped from his seat and was about to run down to help Don Quixote off the course, but Becky grabbed his arm. "Hang on," she said, "Someone else will look after him, and I have an idea."

She explained that Don Quixote would make a perfect man for Princess Gigunda.

"But he's in love with Dulcinea!"

Becky looked at him patiently. "Has anyone ever *seen* Dulcinea? All we have to do is convince Don Quixote that Princess Gigunda *is* Dulcinea."

After the races, they found that Don Quixote had been arrested by the lictors and sent to the Lautumiae, which was the Roman jail. They weren't allowed to see the prisoner, so they went in search of Cicero, who was a lawyer and was able to get Quixote out of the Lautumiae on the promise that he would never visit Rome again.

"I regret to the depths of my soul that my parole does not enable me to destroy those demons," Quixote said as he left Rome's town limits.

"Let's not get into that," Becky said. "What we wanted to tell you was that we've found Dulcinea."

The old man's eyes widened in joy. He clutched at his armor-clad heart. "*Mi amor!* Where is she? I must run to her at once!"

"Not just yet," Becky said. "You should know that she's been changed. She doesn't look like she used to."

"Has some evil sorcerer done this?" Quixote demanded.

"Yes!" Jamie interrupted. He was annoyed that Becky had taken charge of everything, and he wanted to add his contribution to the scheme. "The sorcerer was just a head!" he shouted. "A floating head, and a pair of hands! And he wore dark glasses and had no body!"

A shiver of fear passed through him as he remembered the eerie floating head, but the memory of his old terror did not stop his words from spilling out.

Becky gave him a strange look. "Yeah," she said. "That's right."

"He crashed the interface!" Jamie shouted, the words coming to him out of memory.

Don Quixote paid no attention to this, but Becky gave him another look.

"You're not as dumb as you look, Digit," she said.

"I do not care about Dulcinea's appearance," Don Quixote declared, "I love only the goodness that dwells in her *corazón*."

"She's Princess Gigunda!" Jamie shouted, jumping up and down in enthusiasm. "She's been Princess Gigunda all along!"

And so, the children following, Don Quixote ran clanking to where Princess Gigunda waited near Jamie's house, fell down to one knee, and began to kiss and weep over the Princess' hand. The Princess seemed a little surprised by this until Becky told her that she was really the long-lost Dulcinea, changed into a giant by an evil magician, although she probably didn't remember it because that was part of the spell, too.

So while the Don and the Princess embraced, kissed, and began to warble a love duet, Becky turned to Jamie.

"What's that stuff about the floating head?" she asked. "Where did you come up with that?"

"I dunno," Jamie said. He didn't want to talk about his memory of his family being turned to stone, the eerie glowing figure floating before them. He didn't want to remember how everyone said it was just a dream.

He didn't want to talk about the suspicions that had never quite gone away.

"That stuff was weird, Digit," Becky said. "It gave me the creeps. Let me know before you start talking about stuff like that again."

"Why do you call me Digit?" Jamie asked. Becky smirked.

"No reason," she said.

"Jamie's home!" Mister Jeepers' voice warbled from the sky. Jamie looked up to see Mister Jeepers doing joyful aerial loops overhead. "Master Jamie's home at last!"

"Where shall we go?" Jamie asked.

Their lessons for the day were over, and he and Becky were leaving the little red schoolhouse. Becky, as usual, had done very well on her lessons, better than her older brother, and Jamie felt a growing sense of annoyance. At least he was still better at Latin and computer science.

"I dunno," Becky said. "Where do you want to go?"

"How about Pandaland? We could ride the Whoosh Machine."

Becky wrinkled her face. "I'm tired of that kid stuff," she said.

Jamie looked at her. "But you're a kid."

"I'm not as little as you, Digit," Becky said.

Jamie glared. This was too much. "You're my little sister! I'm bigger than you!"

"No, you're not," Becky said. She stood before him, her arms flung out in exasperation. "Just *notice something* for once, will you?"

Jamie bit back on his temper and looked, and he saw that Becky was, in fact, bigger than he was. And older-looking. Puzzlement replaced his fading anger.

"How did you get so big?" Jamie asked.

"I grew. And you *didn't* grow. Not as fast anyway."

"I don't understand."

Becky's lip curled. "Ask Mom or Dad. Just *ask* them." Her expression turned stony. "But don't believe everything they tell you."

"What do you mean?"

Becky looked angry for a moment, and then her expression relaxed. "Look," she said, "just go to Pandaland and have fun, okay? You don't need me for that. I want to go and make some calls to my friends."

"*What* friends?"

Becky looked angry again. "*My* friends. It doesn't matter who they are!"

"Fine!" Jamie shouted. "I can have fun by myself!"

Becky turned and began to walk home, her legs scissoring against the background of the green grass. Jamie glared after her, then turned and began the walk to Pandaland.

He did all his favorite things, rode the Ferris wheel and the Whoosh Machine, watched Rizzio the Strongman and the clowns. He enjoyed himself, but his enjoyment felt hollow. He found himself *watching*, watching himself at play, watching himself enjoying the rides.

Watching himself not grow as fast as his little sister.

Watching himself wondering whether or not to ask his parents about why that was.

He had the idea that he wouldn't like their answers.

He didn't see as much of Becky after that. They would share lessons, and then Becky would lock herself in her room to talk to her friends on the phone.

Becky didn't have a telephone in her room, though. He looked once when she wasn't there.

After a while, Becky stopped accompanying him for lessons. She'd got ahead of him on everything except Latin, and it was too hard for Jamie to keep up.

After that, he hardly saw Becky at all. But when he saw her, he saw that she was still growing fast. Her clothing was different, and her hair. She'd started wearing makeup.

He didn't know whether he liked her anymore or not.

It was Jamie's birthday. He was eleven years old, and Momma and Daddy and Becky had all come for a party. Don Quixote and Princess Gigunda serenaded Jamie from outside the window, accompanied by La Duchesa on Spanish guitar. There was a big cake with eleven candles. Momma gave Jamie a chart of the stars. When he touched a star, a voice would appear telling Jamie about the star, and lines would appear on the chart showing any constellation the star happened to belong to. Daddy gave Jamie a car, a miniature Mercedes convertible, scaled to Jamie's size, which he could drive around the country and which he could use in the Circus Maximus when the chariots weren't racing.

His sister gave Jamie a kind of lamp stand that would project lights and moving patterns on the walls and ceiling when the lights were off. "Listen to music when you use it," she said.

"Thank you, Becky," Jamie said.

"Becca," she said. "My name is Becca now. Try to remember."

"Okay," Jamie said. "Becca."

Becky—Becca—looked at Momma. "I'm dying for a cigarette," she said. "Can I go, uh, out for a minute?"

Momma hesitated, but Daddy looked severe. "Becca," she said, "this is *Jamie's birthday*. We're all here to celebrate. So why don't we all eat some cake and have a nice time?"

"It's not even real cake," Becca said. "It doesn't *taste* like real cake."

"It's a *nice cake*," Daddy insisted. "Why don't we talk about this later? Let's just have a special time for Jamie."

Becca stood up from the table. "For *the Digit*?" she said. "Why are we having a good time for *Jamie*? He's not even a *real person!*" She thumped herself on the chest. "I'm a *real* person!" she shouted. "Why don't we ever have special times for *me*?"

But Daddy was on his feet by that point and shouting, and Momma was trying to get everyone to be quiet, and Becca was shouting back, and suddenly a determined look entered her face and she just disappeared— suddenly, she wasn't there anymore, there was just only air.

Jamie began to cry. So did Momma. Daddy paced up and down and swore, and then he said, "I'm going to go get her." Jamie was afraid he'd disappear like Becca, and he gave a cry of despair, but Daddy didn't disappear, he just stalked out of the dining room and slammed the door behind him.

Momma pulled Jamie onto her lap and hugged him. "Don't worry, Jamie," she said. "Becky just did that to be mean."

"What happened?" Jamie asked.

"Don't worry about it." Momma stroked his hair. "It was just a mean trick."

"She's growing up," Jamie said. "She's grown faster than me and I don't understand."

"Wait till Daddy gets back," Momma said, "and we'll talk about it."

But Daddy was clearly in no mood for talking when he returned, without Becca. "We're going to have *fun*," he snarled, and reached for the knife to cut the cake.

The cake tasted like ashes in Jamie's mouth. When the Don and Princess Gigunda, Mister Jeepers, and Rizzio the Strongman came into the dining room and sang "Happy Birthday," it was all Jamie could do to hold back the tears.

Afterwards, he drove his new car to the Circus Maximus and drove as fast as he could on the long oval track. The car really wouldn't go very fast. The bleachers on either side were empty, and so was the blue sky above.

Maybe it was a puzzle, he thought, like Princess Gigunda's love life. Maybe all he had to do was follow the right clue, and everything would be fine.

What's the moral they're trying to teach? he wondered.

But all he could do was go in circles, around and around the empty stadium.

"Hey, Digit. Wake up."

Jamie came awake suddenly, with a stifled cry. The room whirled around him. He blinked, realized that the whirling came from the colored lights projected by his birthday present, Becca's lamp stand.

Becca was sitting on his bedroom chair, a cigarette in her hand. Her feet, in the steel-capped boots she'd been wearing lately, were propped up on the bed.

"Are you awake, Jamie?" It was Selena's voice. "Would you like me to sing you a lullaby?"

"Fuck off, Selena," Becca said. "Get out of here. Get lost."

Selena cast Becca a mournful look, then sailed backwards, out the window, riding a beam of moonlight to her pale home in the sky. Jamie watched her go, and felt as if a part of himself was going with her, a part that he would never see again.

"Selena and the others have to do what you tell them, mostly," Becca said. "Of course, Mom and Dad wouldn't tell *you* that."

Jamie looked at Becca. "What's happening?" he said. "Where did you go today?"

Colored lights swam over Becca's face. "I'm sorry if I spoiled your birthday, Digit. I just got tired of the lies, you know? They'd kill me if they knew I was here now, talking to you."

Becca took a draw on her cigarette, held her breath for a second or two, then exhaled. Jamie didn't see or taste any smoke.

"You know what they wanted me to do?" she said. "Wear a little girl's body, so I wouldn't look any older than you, and keep you company in that stupid school for seven hours a day." She shook her head. "I wouldn't do it. They yelled and yelled, but I was damned if I would."

"I don't understand."

Becca flicked invisible ashes off her cigarette, and looked at Jamie for a long time. Then she sighed.

"Do you remember when you were in the hospital?" she said.

Jamie nodded. "I was really sick."

"I was so little then, I don't really remember it very well," Becca said. "But the point is—" She sighed again. "The point is that you weren't getting well. So they decided to—" She shook her head. "Dad took advantage of his position at the University, and the fact that he's been a big doner. They were doing AI research, and the neurology department was into brain modeling, and they needed a test subject, and—Well, the idea is, they've got some of your tissue, and when they get cloning up and running, they'll put you back in—" She saw Jamie's stare, then shook her head.

"I'll make it simple, okay?"

She took her feet off the bed and leaned closer to Jamie. A shiver ran up his back at her expression. "They made a copy of you. An *electronic* copy. They scanned your brain and built a holographic model of it inside a computer, and they put it in a virtual environment, and—" She sat back, took a drag on her cigarette. "And here you are," she said.

Jamie looked at her. "I don't understand."

Colored lights gleamed in Becca's eyes. "You're in a computer, okay? And you're a program. You know what that is, right? From computer class? And the program is sort of in the shape of your mind. Don Quixote and Princess Gigunda are programs, too. And Mrs. Winkle down at the schoolhouse is *usually* a program, but if she needs to teach something complex, then she's an education major from the University."

Jamie felt as if he'd just been hollowed out, a void inside his ribs. "I'm not real?" he said. "I'm not a person?"

"Wrong," Becca said. "You're real, alright. You're the apple of our parents' eye." Her tone was bitter. "Programs are real things," she said, "and yours was a real hack, you know, absolute cutting-edge state-of-the-art technoshit. And the computer that you're in is real, too—I'm interfaced with it right now, down in the family room—we have to wear suits with sensors and a helmet with scanners and stuff. I hope to fuck they don't hear me talking to you down here."

"But what—" Jamie swallowed hard. How could he swallow if he was just a string of code? "What happened to *me*? The original me?"

Becca looked cold. "Well," she said, "you had cancer. You died."

"Oh." A hollow wind blew through the void inside him.

"They're going to bring you back. As soon as the clone thing works out—but this is a government computer you're in, and there are all these government restrictions on cloning, and—"

She shook her head. "Look, Digit," she said. "You really need to know this stuff, okay?"

"I understand." Jamie wanted to cry. But only real people cried, he thought, and he wasn't real. He wasn't real.

"The program that runs this virtual environment is huge, okay, and you're a big program, and the University computer is used for a lot of research, and a lot of the research has a higher priority than you do. So you don't run in real-time—that's why I'm growing faster than you are.

"I'm spending more hours being me than you are. And the parents—" She rolled her eyes. "They aren't making this any better, with their emphasis on *normal family life*."

She sucked on her cigarette, then stubbed it out in something invisible. "See, they want us to be this *normal family*. So we have breakfast together every day, and dinner every night, and spend the evening at the Zoo or in Pandaland or someplace. But the dinner that we eat with *you* is virtual, it doesn't taste like anything—the grant ran out before they got that part of the interface right—so we eat this fast-food crap before we interface with you, and then have dinner all *over* again with *you* . . . Is this making any sense? Because Dad has a job and Mom has a job and I go to school and have friends and stuff, so we really can't get together every night. So they just close your program file, shut it right down, when they're not available to interface with you as what Dad calls a 'family unit,' and that means that there are a lot of hours, days sometimes, when you're just *not running*, you might as well really be *dead*—" She blinked. "Sorry," she said. "Anyway, we're all getting older a lot faster than you are, and it's not fair to you, that's what I think. Especially because the University computer runs fastest at night, because people don't use them as much then, and you're pretty much real-time then, so interfacing with you would be almost normal, but Mom and Dad sleep then, cuz they have day jobs, and they can't have you running around unsupervised in here, for God's sake, they think it's unsafe or something . . . "

She paused, then reached into her shirt pocket for another cigarette. "Look," she said, "I'd better get out of here before they figure out I'm talking to you. And then they'll pull my access codes or something." She stood, brushed something off her jeans. "Don't tell the parents about this stuff right away. Otherwise they must might erase you, and load a backup that doesn't know shit. Okay?"

And she vanished, as she had that afternoon.

Jamie sat in the bed, hugging his knees. He could feel his heart beating in the darkness. How can a program have a heart? he wondered.

Dawn slowly encroached upon the night, and then there was Mister Jeepers, turning lazy cartwheels in the air, his red face leering in the window.

"Jamie's awake!" he said. "Jamie's awake and ready for a new day!"

"Fuck off," Jamie said, and buried his face in the blanket.

Jamie asked to learn more about computers and programming. Maybe, he thought, he could find clues there, he could solve the puzzle. His parents agreed, happy to let him follow his interests.

After a few weeks, he moved into El Castillo. He didn't tell anyone he was going, he just put some of his things in his car, took them up to a tower room, and threw them down on the bed he found there. His Mom came to find him when he didn't come home for dinner.

"It's dinnertime, Jamie," she said. "Didn't you hear the dinner bell?"

"I'm going to stay here for a while," Jamie said.

"You're going to get hungry if you don't come home for dinner."

"I don't need food," Jamie said.

His Mom smiled brightly. "You need food if you're going to keep up with the Whirlikins," she said.

Jamie looked at her. "I don't care about that kid stuff anymore," he said.

When his mother finally turned and left, Jamie noticed that she moved like an old person.

After a while, he got used to the hunger that was programmed into him. It was always *there*, he was always aware of it, but he got so he could ignore it after awhile.

But he couldn't ignore the need to sleep. That was just built into the program, and eventually, try though he might, he needed to give in to it.

He found out he could order the people in the castle around, and he amused himself by making them stand in embarrassing positions, or stand on their head and sing, or form human pyramids for hours and hours.

Sometimes he made them fight, but they weren't very good at it.

He couldn't make Mrs. Winkle at the schoolhouse do whatever he wanted, though, or any of the people who were supposed to teach him things. When it was time for a lesson, Princess Gigunda turned up. She wouldn't follow his orders, she'd just pick him up and carry him to the little red schoolhouse and plunk him down in his seat.

"You're not real!" he shouted, kicking in her arms. "You're not real! And *I'm* not real, either!"

But they made him learn about the world that *was* real, about geography and geology and history, although none of it mattered here.

After the first couple times Jamie had been dragged to school, his father met him outside the schoolhouse at the end of the day.

"You need some straightening out," he said. He looked grim. "You're part of a family. You belong with us. You're not going to stay in the castle anymore, you're going to have a *normal family life.*"

"No!" Jamie shouted. "I like the castle!"

Dad grabbed him by the arm and began to drag him homeward. Jamie called him a *pendejo* and a *fellator*.

"I'll punish you if I have to," his father said.

"How are you going to do that?" Jamie demanded. "You gonna erase my file? Load a backup?"

A stunned expression crossed his father's face. His body seemed to go through a kind of stutter, and the grip on Jamie's arm grew nerveless. Then his face flushed with anger. "What do you mean?" he demanded. "Who told you this?"

Jamie wrenched himself free of Dad's weakened grip. "I figured it out by myself," Jamie said. "It wasn't hard. I'm not a kid anymore."

"I—" His father blinked, and then his face hardened. "You're still coming home."

Jamie backed away. "I want some changes!" he said. "I don't want to be shut off all the time."

Dad's mouth compressed to a thin line. "It was Becky who told you this, wasn't it?"

Jamie felt an inspiration. "It was Mister Jeepers! There's a flaw in his programming! He answers whatever question I ask him!"

Jamie's father looked uncertain. He held out his hand. "Let's go home," he said. "I need to think about this."

Jamie hesitated. "Don't erase me," he said. "Don't load a backup. Please. I don't want to die *twice*."

Dad's look softened. "I won't."

"I want to grow up," Jamie said. "I don't want to be a little kid forever."

Dad held out his hand again. Jamie thought for a moment, then took the hand. They walked over the green grass toward the white frame house on the hill.

"Jamie's home!" Mister Jeepers floated overhead, turning aerial cartwheels. "Jamie's home at last!"

A spasm of anger passed through Jamie at the sight of the witless grin. He pointed at the ground in front of him.

"Crash right here!" he ordered. "*Fast!*"

Mister Jeepers came spiraling down, an expression of comic terror on his face, and smashed to the ground where Jamie pointed. Jamie pointed at the sight of the crumpled body and laughed.

"Jamie's home at last!" Mister Jeepers said.

As soon as Jamie could, he got one of the programmers at the University to fix him up a flight program like the one Mister Jeepers had been using. He swooped and soared, zooming like a super hero through the sky, stunting between the towers of El Castillo and soaring over upturned, wondering faces in the Forum.

He couldn't seem to go as fast as he really wanted. When he started increasing speed, all the scenery below paused in its motion for a second or two, then jumped forward with a jerk. The software couldn't refresh the scenery fast enough to match his speed. It felt strange, because throughout his flight he could feel the wind on his face.

So this, he thought, was why his car couldn't go fast.

So he decided to climb high. He turned his face to the blue sky and went straight up. The world receded, turned small. He could see the Castle, the hills of Whirlikin Country, the crowded Forum, the huge oval of the Circus Maximus. It was like a green plate, with a fuzzy, nebulous horizon where the sky started.

And, right in the center, was the little two-story frame house where he'd grown up.

It was laid out below him like scenery in a snow globe.

After a while he stopped climbing. It took him a while to realize it, because he still felt the wind blowing in his face, but the world below stopped getting smaller.

He tried going faster. The wind blasted onto him from above, but his position didn't change. He'd reached the limits of his world. He couldn't get any higher.

Jamie flew out to the edges of the world, to the horizon. No matter how he urged his program to move, he couldn't make his world fade away.

He was trapped inside the snow globe, and there was no way out.

It was quite a while before Jamie saw Becca again. She picked her way through the labyrinth beneath El Castillo to his throne room, and Jamie slowly materialized atop his throne of skulls.

She didn't appear surprised.

"I see you've got a little Dark Lord thing going here," she said.

"It passes the time," Jamie said.

"And all those pits and stakes and tripwires?"

"Death traps."

"Took me forever to get in here, Digit. I kept getting de-rezzed."

Jamie smiled. "That's the idea."

"Whirlikins as weapons," she nodded. "That was a good one. Bored a hole right through me, the first time."

"Since I'm stuck living here," Jamie said, "I figure I might as well be in charge of the environment. Some of the student programmers at the University helped me with some cool effects."

Screams echoed through the throne room. Fires leaped out of pits behind him. The flames illuminated a form of Marcus Tullius Cicero, who hung crucified above a sea of flame.

"*O tempora, o mores!*" moaned Cicero.

Becca nodded. "Nice," she said. "Not my scene exactly, but nice."

"Since I can't leave," Jamie said, "I want a say in who gets to visit. So either you wait till I'm ready to talk to you, or you take your chances on the death traps."

"Well. Looks like you're sitting pretty, then."

Jamie shrugged. Flames belched. "I'm getting bored with it. I might just wipe it all out and build another place to live in. I can't tell you the number of battles I've won, the number of kingdoms I've trampled. In this reality and others. It's all the same after a while." He looked at her. "You've grown."

"So have you."

"Once the paterfamilias finally decided to allow it." He smiled. "We still have dinner together sometimes, in the old house. Just a normal family, as Dad says. Except that sometimes I turn up in the form of a werewolf, or a giant, or something."

"So they tell me."

"The advantage of being software is that I can look like anything I want. But that's the disadvantage, too, because I can't really become something else, I'm still just . . . me. I may wear another program as a disguise, but I'm still the same program inside, and I'm not a good enough programmer to mess with that, yet." Jamie hopped off his throne, walked a nervous little circle around his sister. "So what brings you to the old neighborhood?" he asked. "The old folks said you were off visiting Aunt Maddy in the country."

"*Exiled*, they mean. I got knocked up, and after the abortion they sent me to Maddy. She was supposed to keep me under control, except she didn't." She picked an invisible piece of lint from her sweater. "So now I'm back." She looked at him. "I'm skipping a lot of the story, but I figure you wouldn't be interested."

"Does it have to do with sex?" Jamie asked. "I'm sort of interested in sex, even though I can't do it, and they're not likely to let me."

"*Let* you?"

"It would require a lot of new software and stuff. I was prepubescent when my brain structures were scanned, and the program isn't set up for making me a working adult, with adult desires et cetera. Nobody was thinking about putting me through adolescence at the time. And the administrators at the University told me that it was very unlikely that anyone was going to give them a grant so that a computer program could have sex." Jamie shrugged. "I don't miss it, I guess. But I'm sort of curious."

Surprise crossed Becca's face. "But there are all kinds of simulations, and . . . "

"They don't work for me, because my mind isn't structured so as to be able to achieve pleasure that way. I can manipulate the programs, but it's about as exciting as working a virtual butter churn." Jamie shrugged again. "But that's okay. I mean, I don't *miss* it. I can always give myself a jolt to the pleasure center if I want."

"Not the same thing," Becca said. "I've done both."

"I wouldn't know."

"I'll tell you about sex if you want," Becca said, "but that's not why I'm here."

"Yes?"

Becca hesitated. Licked her lips. "I guess I should just say it, huh?" she said. "Mom's dying. Pancreatic cancer."

Jamie felt sadness well up in his mind. Only electrons, he thought, moving from one place to another. It was nothing real. He was programmed to feel an analog of sorrow, and that was all.

"She looks normal to me," he said, "when I see her." But that didn't mean anything: his mother chose what she wanted him to see, just as he chose a mask—a werewolf, a giant—for her.

And in neither case did the disguise at all matter. For behind the werewolf was a program that couldn't alter its parameters; and behind the other, ineradicable cancer.

Becca watched him from slitted eyes. "Dad wants her to be scanned, and come here. So we can still be a *normal family* even after she dies."

Jamie was horrified. "Tell her *no*," he said. "Tell her she can't come!"

"I don't think she wants to. But Dad is very insistent."

"She'll be here *forever*! It'll be awful!"

Becca looked around. "Well, she wouldn't do much for your Dark Lord act, that's for sure. I'm sure Sauron's mom didn't hang around the Dark Tower, nagging him about the unproductive way he was spending his time."

Fires belched. The ground trembled. Stalactites rained down like arrows.

"That's not it," Jamie said. "She doesn't want to be here no matter what I'm doing, no matter where I live. Because whatever this place looks like, it's a prison." Jamie looked at his sister. "I don't want my mom in a prison."

Leaping flames glittered in Becca's eyes. "You can change the world you live in," she said. "That's more than I can do."

"But I can't," Jamie said. "I can change the way it *looks*, but I can't change anything *real*. I'm a program, and a program is an *artifact*. I'm a piece of *engineering*. I'm a simulation, with simulated sensory organs that interact with simulated environments—I can only interact with *other artifacts*. *None* of it's real. I don't know what the real world looks or feels or tastes like, I only know what simulations tell me they're *supposed* to taste like. And I can't change any of my parameters unless I mess with the engineering, and I can't do that unless the programmers agree, and even when that happens, I'm still as artificial as I was before. And the computer I'm in is old and clunky, and soon nobody's going to run my operating system anymore, and I'll not only be an artifact, I'll be a museum piece."

"There are other artificial intelligences out there," Becca said. "I keep hearing about them."

"I've talked to them. Most of them aren't very interesting—it's like talking to a dog, or maybe to very intelligent microwave oven. And they've scanned some people in, but those were adults, and all they wanted to do, once they got inside, was to escape. Some of them went crazy."

Becca gave a twisted smile. "I used to be so jealous of you, you know. You lived in this beautiful world, no pollution, no violence, no shit on the streets."

Flames belched.

"*Integra mens augustissima possessio,*" said Cicero.

"Shut up!" Jamie told him. "What the fuck do you know?"

Becca shook her head. "I've seen those old movies, you know? Where somebody gets turned into a computer program, and next thing you know he's in every computer in the world, and running everything?"

"I've seen those, too. Ha ha. Very funny. Shows you what people know about programs."

"Yeah. Shows you what they know."

"I'll talk to Mom," Jamie said.

Big tears welled out of Mom's eyes and trailed partway down her face, then disappeared. The scanners paid a lot of attention to eyes and mouths, for the sake of transmitting expression, but didn't always pick up the things between.

"I'm sorry," she said. "We didn't think this is how it would be."

"Maybe you should have given it more thought," Jamie said.

It isn't sorrow, he told himself again. It's just electrons moving.

"You were such a beautiful baby." Her lower lip trembled. "We didn't want to lose you. They said that it would only be a few years before they could implant your memories in a clone."

Jamie knew all that by now. Knew that the technology of reading memories turned out to be much, much simpler than implanting them—it had been discovered that the implantation had to be made while the brain was actually growing. And government restrictions on human cloning had made tests next to impossible, and the team that had started his project had split up years ago, some to higher-paying jobs, some retired, others to pet projects of their own. How his father had long ago used up whatever pull he'd had at the University trying to keep everything together. And how he long ago had acquired or purchased patents and copyrights for the whole scheme, except for Jamie's program, which was still owned jointly by the University and the family.

Tears reappeared on Mom's lower face, dripped off her chin. "There's potentially a lot of money at stake, you know. People want to raise perfect children. Keep them away from bad influences, make sure that they're raised free from violence."

"So they want to control the kid's entire environment," Jamie said.

"Yes. And make it *safe*. And wholesome. And—"

"Just like *normal family life*," Jamie finished. "No diapers, no vomit, no messes. No having to interact with the kid when the parents are tired. And then you just download the kid into an adult body, give him a diploma, and kick him out of the house. And call yourself a perfect parent."

"And there are *religious people* . . . " Mom licked her lips. "Your Dad's been talking to them. They want to raise children in environments that reflect their beliefs completely. Places where there is no temptation, no sin. No science or ideas that contradict their own . . . "

"But Dad isn't religious," Jamie said.

"These people have money. Lots of money." Mom reached out, took his hand. Jamie thought about all the code that enabled her to do it, that enabled them both to feel the pressure of unreal flesh on unreal flesh.

"I'll do what you wish, of course," she said. "I don't have that desire for immortality, the way your father does." She shook her head. "But I don't know what your father will do once his time comes."

The world was a disk a hundred meters across, covered with junk: old Roman ruins, gargoyles fallen from a castle wall, a broken chariot, a shattered bell. Outside the rim of the world, the sky was black, utterly black, without a ripple or a star.

Standing in the center of the world was a kind of metal tree with two forked, jagged arms.

"Hi, Digit," Becca said.

A dull fitful light gleamed on the metal tree, as if it were reflecting a bloody sunset.

"Hi, sis," it said.

"Well," Becca said. "We're alone now."

"I caught the notice of Dad's funeral. I hope nobody missed me."

"I missed you, Digit." Becca sighed. "Believe it or not."

"I'm sorry."

Becca restlessly kicked a piece of junk, a hubcap from an old, miniature car. It clanged as it found new lodgement in the rubble. "Can you appear as a person?" she asked. "It would make it easier to talk to you."

"I've finished with all that," Jamie said. "I'd have to resurrect too much dead programming. I've cut the world down to next to nothing, I've got rid of my body, my heartbeat, the sense of touch."

"All the human parts," Becca said sadly.

The dull red light oozed over the metal tree like a drop of blood. "Everything except sleep and dreams. It turns out that sleep and dreams have too much to do with the way people process memory. I can't get rid of them, not without cutting out too much of my mind." The tree gave a strange, disembodied laugh. "I dreamed about you, the other day. And about Cicero. We were talking Latin."

"I've forgotten all the Latin I ever knew." Becca tossed her hair, forced a laugh. "So what do you do nowadays?"

"Mostly I'm a conduit for data. The University has been using me as a research spider, which I don't mind doing, because it passes the time. Except that I take up a lot more memory than any *real* search spider, and don't do that much better a job. And the information I find doesn't have much to do with *me*—it's all about the real world. The world I can't touch." The metal tree bled color.

"Mostly," he said, "I've just been waiting for Dad to die. And now it's happened."

There was a moment of silence before Becca spoke. "You know that dad had himself scanned before he went."

"Oh yeah. I knew."

"He set up some kind of weird foundation that I'm not part of, with his patents and programs and so on, and his money and some other people's."

"He'd better not turn up here."

Becca shook her head. "He won't. Not without your permission, anyway. Because I'm in charge here. You—your program—it's not a part of the foundation. Dad couldn't get it all, because the University has an interest, and so does the family." There was a moment of silence. "And I'm the family now."

"So you . . . *inherited* me," Jamie said. Cold scorn dripped from his words.

"That's right," Becca said. She squatted down amid the rubble, rested her forearms on her knees.

"What do you want me to do, Digit? What can I do to make it better for you?"

"No one ever asked me that," Jamie said.

There was another long silence.

"Shut it off," Jamie said. "Close the file. Erase it."

Becca swallowed hard. Tears shimmered in her eyes. "Are you sure?" she asked.

"Yes. I'm sure."

"And if they ever perfect the clone thing? If we could make you . . . " She took a breath. "A person?"

"No. It's too late. It's . . . not something I can want anymore."

Becca stood. Ran a hand through her hair. "I wish you could meet my daughter," she said. "Her name is Christy. She's a real beauty."

"You can bring her," Jamie said.

Becca shook her head. "This place would scare her. She's only three. I'd only bring her if we could have . . . "

"The old environment," Jamie finished. "Pandaland. Mister Jeepers. Whirlikin Country."

Becca forced a smile. "Those were happy days," she said. "They really were. I was jealous of you, I know, but when I look back at that time . . . " She wiped tears with the back of her hand. "It was the best."

"Virtual environments are nice places to visit, I guess," Jamie said. "But you don't want to live in one. Not forever." Becca looked down at her feet, planted amid rubble.

"Well," she said. "If you're sure about what you want."

"I am."

She looked up at the metal form, raised a hand. "Goodbye, Jamie," she said.

"Goodbye," he said.

She faded from the world.

And in time, the world and the tree faded, too.

Hand in hand, Daddy and Jamie walked to Whirlikin Country. Jamie had never seen the Whirlikins before, and he laughed and laughed as the Whirlikins spun beneath their orange sky.

The sound of a bell rang over the green hills. "Time for dinner, Jamie," Daddy said.

Jamie waved goodbye to the Whirlikins, and he and Daddy walked briskly over the fresh green grass toward home.

"Are you happy, Jamie?" Daddy asked.

"Yes, Daddy!" Jamie nodded. "I only wish Momma and Becky could be here with us."

"They'll be here soon."

When, he thought, they can get the simulations working properly.

Because *this* time, he thought, there would be no mistakes. The foundation he'd set up before he died had finally purchased the University's interest in Jamie's program—they funded some scholarships, that was all it finally took. There was no one in the Computer Department who had an interest anymore.

Jamie had been loaded from an old backup—there was no point in using the corrupt file that Jamie had become, the one that had turned itself into a *tree*, for heaven's sake.

The old world was up and running, with a few improvements. The foundation had bought their own computer—an old one, so it wasn't too expensive—that would run the environment full time. Some other children might be scanned, to give Jamie some playmates and peer socialization.

This time it would work, Daddy thought. Because this time, Daddy was a program too, and he was going to be here every minute, making sure that the environment was correct and that everything went exactly according to plan. That he and Jamie and everyone else had a normal family life, perfect and shining and safe.

And if the clone program ever worked out, they would come into the real world again. And if downloading into clones was never perfected, then they would stay here.

There was nothing wrong with the virtual environment. It was a *good* place.

Just like normal family life. Only forever.

And when this worked out, the foundation's backers—fine people, even if they did have some strange religious ideas—would have their own environments up and running. With churches, angels, and perhaps even the presence of God . . .

"Look!" Daddy said, pointing. "It's Mister Jeepers!"

Mister Jeepers flew off the rooftop and spun happy spirals in the air as he swooped toward Jamie. Jamie dropped Daddy's hand and ran laughing to greet his friend.

"Jamie's home!" Mister Jeepers cried. "Jamie's home at last!"

First published in *Not of Woman Born,* edited by Constance Ash, 1999.

ABOUT THE AUTHOR

Walter Jon Williams is an award-winning author who has been listed on the best-seller lists of the *New York Times* and the *Times* of London. He is the author of twenty-seven novels and three collections of short fiction, *Frankenstein and Other Foreign Devils, Facets,* and *The Green Leopard Plague and Other Stories.* In 2001 he won a Nebula Award for his novelette, "Daddy's World," and won again in 2005 for "The Green Leopard Plague." His novels include *Aristoi, Hardwired, Days of Attonment, Voice of the Whirlwind, House of Shards, Metropolitan, City On Fire, The Praxis, The Sundering, Conventions of War, This Is Not a Game,* and *Deep State.* He has also written for George RR Martin's Wild Cards project, for comics, the screen, and for television, and has worked in the gaming world, where he scripted the mega-hit Spore. His latest work is *The Fourth Wall,* a near-future thriller set in the world of alternate reality gaming.

A Dance with Futuristic Dragons: The Science-Fantasy Glamour of Marc Bolan and T. Rex

JASON HELLER

"Get it on. Bang a gong. Get it on."

These simple lyrics are Marc Bolan's calling card—at least in the United States, where the 1971 song "Get It On (Bang a Gong)" became the lone hit by Marc Bolan's band T. Rex. A staple of classic-rock radio, "Get It On" is not the type of song that threatened to storm the rarified heights of the poetic canon. A slinky affair full of sly rhythm and stomping riffs, "Get It On" wormed its way into the ears of America—Bolan had already established himself as a superstar in his native England—like some unholy progeny of heavy metal and bubblegum pop. Glam rock, the genre he helped create, was launched into a loftier orbit by David Bowie, his friend, rival, and closest contemporary. But unlike Bowie's angst-ridden tales about his alien alter ego Ziggy Stardust and the lost astronaut Major Tom, Bolan was happy to write bouncy nonsense.

Dig a little deeper into "Get It On," however, and there's something far more fantastic at play. Amid his blunt entreaties for sex, Bolan sprinkles a curious assortment of heady non-sequiturs. "You got the teeth of the Hydra upon you," goes one line; "With your cloak full of eagles," goes another. These aren't the brute come-ons of your typical '70s cock-rock song. They're phrases that could have appeared in a book of high fantasy—a term coined in 1971 by Lloyd Alexander, author of the fantasy epic *The Chronicles of Prydain*—or even a spirited session of *Chainmail*, the groundbreaking fantasy role-playing game that was co-created by future *Dungeons & Dragons* icon Gary Gygax and released in 1971, just as "Get It On" was ascending the pop charts.

135

As it turns out, Bowie wasn't the only major glam-rock star in the early '70s who flaunted an appreciation for—and an appropriation of—speculative fiction. It may not be immediately obvious from "Get It On," but Bolan is one of the 20th century's foremost unifiers of popular music and fantasy (and to a lesser degree, science fiction—or more precisely, the hybrid subgenre of science-fantasy, which better suited Bolan's romantic view of the cosmos). His appreciation wasn't a passing fancy or part of some fad. Taken as a whole, Bolan's body of work—if not his entire life, cut short as it was in 1977 at the age of 29—was an extended, elaborate narrative spun of myth and magic.

Fantasy was in Marc Bolan's bones.

In the London borough of Hackney in 1955, eight-year-old Mark Feld lay in bed with the measles. Ill though he was, he wasn't alone. The boy was surrounded by dinosaurs, the inhabitants of books on prehistoric creatures that his parents, of limited means but always indulgent of their two sons, had given him. Those dinosaurs "were like dragons that could have breathed fire and smoke," he later reminisced, long after changing his name to Marc Bolan, "and somehow, because they existed, they justified unicorns and centaurs and the whole Narnia scene."

C. S. Lewis' *The Chronicles of Narnia*—published between 1950 and 1956, just as the young Mark Feld was learning to read and developed a lifelong love of books—proved to be just one of the many works of speculative fiction that fascinated the boy. Another was the seminal SF short story "A Sound of Thunder" by Ray Bradbury. In particular, the mighty Tyrannosaurus Rex being hunted by time travelers in Bradbury's story lodged in Feld's impressionable mind. To him, dinosaurs again equated to dragons, not to mention the notion that Earth's primordial past was a vast fantasia of strange, preternatural beings.

That notion was driven home by another series of books that captivated Feld: *The Lord of the Rings*. J. R. R. Tolkien's famed fantasy trilogy, plus its predecessor, *The Hobbit*, became the boy's bible. It didn't hurt that Feld was unnaturally small for his age, with cherubic cheeks, curly hair, and a twinkle in his eye, which surely caused him to empathize with Frodo, Bilbo, and the other hobbits of the Shire. (Even as an adult, Feld would never top five-foot-seven.) And of course, *The Hobbit* held a dragon—the fearsome, saurian behemoth that would continue to enthrall Feld after he grew up, changed his name, and remembered "A Sound of Thunder" when dubbing his band Tyrannosaurus Rex (later to be shortened to T. Rex).

Tyrannosaurus Rex formed in 1967, but Bolan—like Bowie— underwent some changes to get there. His first solo single under the name Marc Bolan was released in 1965; it flopped, but its title, "The Wizard," more than hinted at Bolan's unabashed adoration of fantasy literature. "Walking in the woods one day," he sings, "I met a man who said that he was magic." After observing the salient details of the mage's appearance, including the "pointed hat upon his head" and the fact that "shadows followed him all around," Bolan concludes the song with the eerie couplet, "Silver sunlight in his eyes / The wizard turned and melted in the sky." Although not named, the song's titular wizard is a dead ringer for Tolkien's Gandalf.

The failure of "The Wizard," as well as a brief stint in the rock band John's Children, left Bolan directionless—that is, until he reinvented himself as the elfin shaman of the psychedelic folk duo Tyrannosaurus Rex. With percussionist Stephen Ross Porter—renamed Steve Peregrin Took in honor of the hobbit Peregrin Took from *The Lord of the Rings*— the twosome took the hippie aesthetic to a mystical extreme. The pair wore extravagant robes, sat cross-legged on stages as if initiating some sorcerous rite, and began crafting music that evoked the myths, legends, and creatures of some imaginary past. Albums titles such as 1968's *My People Were Fair and Had Sky in Their Hair but Now They're Content to Wear Stars on Their Brows*; 1968's *Prophets, Seers, and Sages, the Angels of the Ages*; and 1969's *Unicorn* drove home Bolan's obsession with fantasy—one every ounce as powerful as Bowie's obsession with science fiction, which was soon to become prominent with his 1969 smash "Space Oddity." According to Peter Doggett's book on Bowie, *The Man Who Sold the World*, Bolan claimed to have written part of "Space Oddity," a claim that's never been corroborated—although Bolan did play guitar on "Prettiest Star," Bowie's next single after "Space Oddity."

In fact, Bolan and Bowie would end up working with the same producer, Tony Visconti—only Bolan came with a condition. He insisted that Visconti read Tolkien before working with him. As Visconti recounts in the 2007 BBC documentary *Marc Bolan: The Final Word*, Bolan told him, "I want you to read *The Lord of the Rings*. Read this if you want to know what I'm about." But Bolan was more than simply obsessed; he was immersed. Visconti adds, "He actually lived [in Tolkien's realm of Middle-earth]. In his mind, that all existed. He saw himself as maybe, possibly, a reincarnation of some bard or some wizard that lived in the time when elves walked the earth." Coincidentally, or perhaps not, Bolan regularly performed in an English nightclub in the late '60s called Middle Earth.

Bolan considered himself "a science fiction writer who sings," presumably using the term "science fiction" as a catch-all for science fiction and fantasy, as was common at the time. He worked on an ultimately unrealized science-fiction rock opera, writing songs for it such as "Brain Police," "Metropolis" (possibly a reference to Fritz Lang's 1927 SF film of the same name, also a favorite of Bowie's), and "Dynamo." He even once told radio interviewer that he had numerous fantasy novels of his own in the works.

One such planned book, *The Children of Rarn*, never came to be, but Bolan had at least thought it through extensively. "It's about prehistoric Earth," he once explained, "before the dinosaurs were heavy creatures. There were two races of people then, the Peacelings and the Dworns, and a third group of beings called Lithons, all locked in complex, antagonistic relationships"—akin to some amalgam of H. G. Wells' *The Time Machine*, with its Eloi and Morlocks, and Hammer Films' popular prehistoric movies of the time, such as 1966's *One Million Years B.C.* Years later, he claimed to have written a book of science fiction stories titled *Wilderness of My Mind*—and although the book has yet to surface, Bolan boastfully claimed that none other than Ray Bradbury, Bolan's formative influence, had shown an interest in it.

That said, Bolan did publish a book. In 1969, his collection of fantasy poetry *Warlock of Love*—a title that might as well have described the robed, spellbinding, sensuous Bolan himself—was released, and it became a cult hit. "Dedicated to the woods of knowledge," it began, and a typical snippet of the text reads like so:

The questical day had held all the promise of an artist,
but with the grey horseless cloud of the autumn
afternoon all hope of starfields revealed was lost, as
a pebble of love in the black scorched deserts of
civilisation.

As a last hermetic gesture, with the masts of the
day spent, the gaunt man, pure of skin but soiled
of soul, prepared his parchment scroll and crouched
like a beggar began the last task of his day—an
etching of a child, blue skinned and shapen like a
fowl of the skies, with eyes so true and hallowed
that the artition wept as he drew, and already the
quest was begun.

Where Bowie peered forward with fear and wonder into humankind's technological tomorrow, Bolan looked backward—even though his mention of "the black scorched deserts of civilization" in *Warlock of Love* alluded to a science-fantasy hybrid, one where an apocalypse, possibly atomic in origin, had cleared the world of science and left room for magic.

The arcadian, folklore-like aura that surrounded Bolan's fantasy-themed music with Tyrannosaurus Rex didn't reach the audience he'd hoped. In an attempt to appeal to a more universal listenership, the band's 1970 album *T. Rex* tinkered with shorter, punchier, electrified songs. Bolan fired Took, hired a more conventional rock band, and shortened the group's name to T. Rex. (Following Took's ouster, the drummer formed a short-lived psychedelic group called Shagrat, named after an orc from *The Lord of the Rings*.)

T. Rex went on to release anthems like "Get It On (Bang a Gong)," thus fulfilling Bolan's ambitions of stardom. But even then, his swaggering riffs and daydream lyrics retained traces of Tyrannosaurus Rex's fantastical vibe. In 1970, Bolan's appearance as a guest guitarist on Bowie's Venusian-populated song "Memory of a Free Festival" was not only one of the points where the two glam titans collided on tape, but where glam rock became a primary vessel for science fiction and fantasy in song—although in a campier, pulpier, more mysteriously playful way than the sober-faced adaptations of those genres happening at the same time in progressive rock. (Venus would pop up again in "Venus Loon," a 1974 song from the T. Rex album *Zinc Alloy and the Hidden Riders of Tomorrow*, itself a cheeky nod to Bowie's more famous fictional band, Ziggy Stardust and the Spiders from Mars.) At one point in the summer of 1974, Bowie and Bolan spent days in a hotel room binge-watching a print of *A Clockwork Orange* that they'd procured, a testament to just how much the science fiction of Stanley Kubrick and Anthony Burgess affected their work. In his book *Electric Eden*, Rob Young observes, "Bolan and Bowie were [. . .] Pied Pipers [. . .], transporting their young listeners from immersion in a speculative, mythological past and repositioning pop music in a future of plastic, glitter, and tin."

Science fiction continued to seep into Bolan's fantasy. Smuggling in references to mythical creatures, space travel, and cosmic awe, T. Rex songs like 1971's "Planet Queen" and the following year's "Ballroom of Mars" lured listeners into a kaleidoscopic, science-fantasy universe of Bolan's construction—all while evoking SF legends like Edgar Rice Burroughs, whose John Carter of Mars series similarly combined fantasy and science fiction into a staggeringly wondrous whole. No T. Rex album exemplifies this better than 1976's *Futuristic Dragon*; the cover depicts Bolan—or a character closely resembling him—riding a smoke-bellowing dragon, like some Celtic warrior of yore going forth to vanquish the cold forces of anachronistic technocracy. (It was painted by the famed artist George Underwood, who was also responsible for the covers of Bowie's *Hunky Dory* and *Ziggy Stardust* as well as numerous science fiction and fantasy novels.)

Futuristic Dragon is by no means a concept album, let alone one entirely adhering to science-fantasy. Songs such as "Jupiter Liar" and "Theme for a Dragon," however, conjure familiar SFF themes—although not as potently as the album's opening track, "Futuristic Dragon (Introduction)." A piece of spoken-word poetry recited over Hendrix-meets-disco weirdness, it sums up Bolan's fantasist fever-dream in a handful of compact, vivid lines:

> Deep beneath an ancient shadow
> Stunned with age and too much wisdom
> Reclined in glass, with eyes too steep
> Relentless dimensions of quadrophonic sleep
> Dwelt the wild grinning cyclopean pagan
> Screaming destruction in sheer dazzling raiment
> A thunderbolt master, a 'lectronic savior

A cold galactic raver, the Futuristic DragonBolan's untimely death in a car crash a year after *Futuristic Dragon*'s release left the sprawling saga that he wove throughout his songs tragically unfinished. Still, Bolan was able to lodge one last plea in favor of the literary genres he so passionately embodied. In his column in the British music magazine *Record Mirror* on September 10, 1977—six days before his death—he penned a glowing review of *Star Wars*, which he'd just seen. In it he wrote, "Now perhaps people will pay more attention to the science fiction field where so many great poets, writers, and musicians are lurking unsung."

Like George Lucas, Marc Bolan preached science fiction and fantasy to the masses. In an era before speculative fiction had become respected and embraced by the mainstream, he smuggled speculative fiction into more popular and palatable forms, easy to digest but still holding true to what makes SFF tick: imagination, spectacle, and a quest for understanding unrestrained by the mundane and banal. In an interview, Bolan was once asked what drove him to become a star—what kept him up there in the limelight besides the obvious worldly rewards of fame and fortune. His response: "On that stage, I'm at liberty. I'm in a realm of fantasy."

ABOUT THE AUTHOR

Jason Heller is a former nonfiction editor of *Clarkesworld;* as part of the magazine's 2012 editorial team, he received a Hugo Award. He is also the author of the alt-history novel *Taft 2012* (Quirk Books) and a Senior Writer for *The Onion's* pop-culture site, *The A.V. Club*. His short fiction has appeared in *Apex Magazine, Sybil's Garage, Farrago's Wainscot,* and others, and his SFF-related reviews and essays have been published in *Weird Tales, Entertainment Weekly NPR.org, Tor.com,* and Ann and Jeff VanderMeer's *The Time Traveler's Almanac* (Tor Books). He lives in Denver with this wife Angie.

The Humble Swashbuckling Grandmaster: A Conversation with Gene Wolfe

KATE BAKER

I first met Gene Wolfe in San Jose, CA in May of 2013. He had just received his well-deserved SFWA Grand Master Award in front of adoring peers and fans. Throughout the weekend, I watched as his autographing line never seemed to diminish, legions of readers eager to have their books signed by a master.

Despite our brief meeting where I handed him a customary gift on behalf of SFWA, he was warm, soft-spoken, and genuinely appreciative of all the attention he had been given. I may be just a brief and smaller shadow in ever growing lines of people Mr. Wolfe has encountered throughout his life, but his writing has left such an indelible mark on so many in the science fiction and fantasy communities.

So when given the opportunity to interview him at World Fantasy in Saratoga, I jumped at the chance. He was thoughtful and took me on many different trips down memory lane. I'm so grateful for the opportunity to speak with him.

The author of over thirty works, Mr. Wolfe has been nominated and won multiple genre awards, has been inducted in the Science Fiction Hall of Fame, has been the guest of honor at many conventions, and his newest novel, *A Borrowed Man*, is out in stores now.

With a critically acclaimed and award-winning writing career spanning multiple decades, what brings you back to the keyboard time after time?

Oh my, it's what I do. Why does the woodpecker peck the galvanized downspout? That's what he does, he's a woodpecker [laugh] and I'm a writer. I started by dictating stories to my mother as a very small child and I couldn't write at that time, I hadn't learned any of that. I had learned to read in a very simple way and I made up stories myself. My mother who knew shorthand took them down and later wrote them out for me.

Is it the thrill of telling a great story?

Yes! Being in the story, the other characters can't see me, but I'm there. I think, gee, does the storm sink the ship or not and so on.

Do you put yourself in a lot of your protagonists?

No, I don't think so, I'm too dull to be a protagonist. Protagonists usually have to do more swashbuckling than I have ever done. I do have a cutlass though.

You do? Have you ever gotten to use it?

No. [laugh] But I look at it and say, wouldn't that be fun?! I like to have those things. My publisher gave me the cutlass when I was writing *Pirate Freedom* and it gives me the feel of what the weapon was like.

This stuff gives you a little peek into the past or whatever it is that you don't get from books.

In the novel Peace, there have been quite a few interpretations of what actually happens to the protagonist, Alden Dennis Weer. While you've made the intentions clear in subsequent interviews, does it ever surprise you when possible unintended theories are mentioned?

No . . . well. I've been doing this too long to be surprised because I've gotten some of the most off-the-wall, incredible interpretations and you look at some of this stuff and it's just . . . crazy, and you think, well, anything is possible. Somebody can look into the story and what they are seeing is themselves.

Did those fantastic interpretations ever give you any new ideas to write?

Oh, no . . . not good ones. Not good ones.

Empathy in the different shoes of a first person perspective takes practice. Is it the easiest method in which to write or the most meaningful?

When you write third person, you remove yourself. It's the distance, it's something I'm seeing on a screen or something. When you have a first person narrator, you are much more into the story. Also, the first person narrator can comment from his viewpoint on actions. If the author comments from his viewpoint, it's usually ruinously bad.

Going back to that first person narrative, you have mentioned that even real people in general are unreliable narrators in their own lives, despite their best intentions. Why is that?

Narrators are always unreliable. There are narrators that are openly unreliable and there are narrators that pretend to be totally reliable. But they are always unreliable because people are writing books and people can't be trusted, you know?

I read that a fan asked you once why there was a dearth of villains in your writing, to which you replied that good people are far more interesting than evil ones. Are you specifically speaking to the choices in light of tough circumstances or overcoming faults?

I think it's the human condition. If they are fictional villains, they have very narrow viewpoints. 'What benefits me?' 'How can I make money out of this?' Or there is just joy in cruelty, which of course exists, but it's a very narrow thing. The thing you have to remember is that a real villain never thinks he's a villain.

You've mentioned in the past your love for H.G. Wells', The Island of Dr. Moreau. Just how many times would you say you've read that book?

To the best of my knowledge, four times. I read it three times in my early teens somewhere and then I started a fourth reading and I realized I knew everything and I said that I'm going to put that aside until I've forgotten it a little bit and then I'll pull it out again. They put the whole novel in an issue of *Famous Fantastic Mysteries* and I didn't actually look at it again until I had to write a piece for a man who was putting together a collection of essays.

Now in your newest novel, A Borrowed Man—E.A. Smithe is a mystery writer brought back without consent as a "reclone." One of the interesting aspects, and I hope not too spoilerific, is that despite being owned and unable to rebel from their current predicament, reclones are unable to produce any new works.

They are not allowed to. That would cloud the issue, you see.

But we've seen from multiple examples, record companies, publishers, etc., bring back "never before seen works!" of artists, authors, and musicians to make more money. Why bring back someone famous that you can't use in that way or exploit?

They would be consumed with their new work instead of talking about their old work and it's talking about their old work that is what they've been brought back to do. You could clone Charles Dickens presumably, dig him up and get some DNA material and get yourself a new Charles Dickens. But, you want him to be there as a reference to the guy who wrote *Oliver Twist* and *A Christmas Carol.*

E.A. Smithe is reborn into a world where every problem seems to be solved. No war, hunger, strife, etc. Yet, as we read on, we realize there are so many things left unsaid about underlying issues. Was there any particular parallel you wished to draw between your 22nd century setting and today?

They definitely have their own problems. That's just reality. Throughout human history, there are always underlying problems. Sometimes we don't realize what they are. The caveman had underlying problems.

I also noticed in A Borrowed Man, the publishing landscape has whittled down to POD only with a large absence of precious hand-held paper books. Is this inevitability, and if so, why?

Yes. I grieve for that. That is part of what makes the civilization presented in that book a dystopia. If we abandon literature, we abandon the best part of the human past.

I see that a sequel is in the works. Interlibrary Loan will follow in the footsteps of your mystery writer protagonist. Can you give us some advanced spoilers?

No, because I haven't finished it yet, and it may not be published, etc. etc. but . . . Smithe is sent to a different library on interlibrary loan and gets mixed up with a cookbook author and so on and so forth.

Do you think you will ever return to the shorter forms, like The Fifth Head of Cerberus?

Yes. Definitely. One of the things I've been promising myself as I try to write this new book is that I'm not going to start a new book after this, I'm going to write a bunch of short stories. Short stories are how you really learn how to do it. I used to believe that [writing short stories] wasn't necessary, and in the strict sense, it isn't necessary, but there are people who taught themselves to write by writing novels. But that's doing something that's already hard with one hand tied behind your back. You are making it that much harder on yourself and the readier path to writing good work and more publishable work is to write short stories. That's why it's so much to our advantage to have short story markets.

There's little left to urge someone to write a short story if it can't be bought and published! Print markets are dwindling, but there are Internet paying markets and one would hope that there are more of them.

Aside from writing short stories and learning the craft, what other piece of advice would you give a new writer?

The main piece of advice that I would give to the new writer is to write. The difference between writers and would-be writers is that would-be writers write very little and writers write a hell of a lot and you learn by doing. You can read three books on swimming, and attend seventeen lectures on swimming but if you've never been in the water . . . you don't know much about swimming.

I have a time machine in my pocket. You can go back to one moment in your life to relive. What is it?

Do I get to stay there?

If you like . . .

Oh wow, okay. I would go back to the moment where I went out of my bedroom on Christmas morning and saw a shiny new bicycle standing beside the Christmas tree. My parents were still alive. I was a kid, and I had life before me. There are things that I would change, but there are an awful lot of things I would just greet with joy. The family dog died when I was at college, when I got that new bicycle, she was still alive and so on and so forth.

All this reminiscing about life and career, did you ever imagine you'd be doing this? Do you believe in fate?

Yes. The completely materialistic view is clearly wrong. The world is full of things you cannot explain, one or two you can pass off as there will be some explanation later when we know more, but when you see how much there is that purely materialistic view cannot explain, you realize that view is only one part of a larger whole. Many people are trying to pretend that view is all there is.

ABOUT THE AUTHOR

Kate Baker is the Podcast Director and Non-fiction Editor for *Clarkesworld Magazine.* She has been very privileged to narrate over three hundred short stories/poems by some of the biggest names in Science Fiction and Fantasy.

Kate lives in Northern Connecticut with her first fans; her three wonderful children. She is currently employed as the Director of Operations for the Science Fiction and Fantasy Writers of America.

Another Word: On Reading, Writing, and the Classics
CAT RAMBO

In many ways I'm glad that I didn't have the Internet when growing up; among them is the effect it had on my reading. I was a rapid reader and I read all over the place, frequently re-reading if it was something interesting or I was driven to it by boredom and lack of other reading material. (Kids, this is the #1 thing to love about the Internet—you can always find something to read nowadays. I even have *The Canterbury Tales* on my phone nowadays for textual emergencies.)

I went through most of my parents' (both educators) shelves, including some oddities like the complete Albee, Tennessee Williams, and Faulkner as well as all of Thurber and Perelman. At my grandparents, I read five gazillion *Reader's Digest* Abridged novels and a bunch of antiquated children's books that included Kingsley's *The Water Babies* and *Little Black Sambo* at one house while at the other, I found a mess of modern literature and my uncle's boxes of pulp fiction, primarily Doc Savage and Remo Williams.

I read everything I could find. At the library, after they finally, reluctantly allowed me down into the adult stacks at twelve, I terrorized myself with H.P. Lovecraft. Then, there were the extremely limited books available the year we spent in Mexico: a mixture of a tiny lending library and the spy and military fiction already there in my bedroom, left there by the owner.

A set of *World Book* encyclopedias as well as an encyclopedia of animals and a coffee table book on wildflowers that taught me how to identify wild trilliums by leaf alone. Gifts from grandparents included the *Lord of the Rings* in the original bootleg edition. I read it all—the wonderful offerings plucked from the pages of Scholastic, the tiny school library with its somewhat outdated collection, and finally, fantasy & science fiction from the Griffon Bookstore.

I read everything the Griffon had, I think, in the F&SF section, particularly since when I was working there it was kosher to sit during slow times and read at the front desk. I also went through a number of the Penguin classics, which were displayed on the shelves closest to the front desk—all of Dickens, Hardy, and a lot of Trollope for one—and a great many Greek and Roman texts. I'm sure many of the nuances escaped me, but I may have also run the only D&D campaign with references to Aristophanes in it.

I was lucky. I read fast and omnivorously. We had basically three TV channels (plus the religious ones). At some point we got Pong, but that was it for video games. When we got one of the first Macintosh computers, it was a revelation and a half.

Later on in college, someone came through and told a bunch of fellow English majors and myself that Notre Dame English grads usually had crappy GRE scores, so I got a basic overview of literature (I remember the title as being *A Biography of English Literature* but I haven't been able to track it down) and used it for my reading list, reading or at least skimming every work the author referenced. That lengthy list included things like George Orwell's, *Keep the Aspidistra Flying*, which is the only reason why I know what an aspidistra is. (I ended up doing well on the GREs, sufficiently so to satisfy my highly competitive soul.)

Despite the fact that the Internet was starting to become a force, I logged a lot of reading time during work hours in college, primarily at the hospital computer lab where I worked and where the long night hours left plenty of time for reading with little other distraction other than the need to change a computer back-up tape every twenty minutes.

The point I want to make about my perspective on the "classics" is that I've read a substantial portion, both of the F&SF variety and the larger set, and made some of them the focus of study in grad school. (Again from both sets, since that focus was an uneasy combination of late 19th/early 20th American lit and cultural studies with a stress on comics/animation. You can see me here pontificating on The Virtual Sublime or here on Tank Girl. I'm not sure I could manage that depth of theory-speak again, at least without some sort of crash course to bring me back up to speed. But I digress.)

So here's the question that brought me here: should fantasy and science fiction readers read the F&SF classics? And the answer is a resounding, unqualified yes, because they are missing out on some great reading in two ways if they don't. How so?

They miss some good books. So many *many* good books. At some point I want to put together an annotated reading list but that's a project for tinkering with in one's retirement, I think. But, for example, I'm reading *The Rediscovery of Man: The Collected Stories of Cordwainer Smith* right now (in tiny chunks, savoring the hell out of it) and they are such good stories, even with the occasional dated bit.

They miss some of the context of contemporary reading, some of the replies those authors are making to what has come before. *The Forever War*, for example, is in part a reply to *Bill the Galactic Hero*; read together, both texts gain more complexity and interest.

Beyond that, they run the risk of accepting regurgitations instead of originality—and I will argue that regurgitation is not a process that makes things better, but simply more digestible by even the simplest and most inexperienced digestive systems. There's a reason we lay aside children's books and move onto more complicated things as our tastes become more sophisticated.

Admittedly, styles of writing change, and old patterns run the risk of alienating readers. I gave a young friend the *Lord of the Rings* and was dismayed when he bounced off it. Despite being a fantasy fan, the long sentences and formal prose put him off. Margaret Cavendish's *The Blazing World* is very early SF (and a charming early example of Mary Sue fiction) but difficult to read because of the antiquated prose style. Here, for example, is a single sentence:

The Lady now finding her self in so strange a place, and amongst such wonderful kind of Creatures, was extreamly strucken with fear, and could entertain no other Thoughts, but that every moment her life was to be a sacrifice to their cruelty; but those Bear-like Creatures, how terrible soever they appear'd to her sight, yet were they so far from exercising any cruelty upon her, that rather they shewed her all civility and kindness imaginable; for she being not able to go upon the Ice, by reason of its slipperiness, they took her up in their rough arms, and carried her into their City, where instead of Houses, they had Caves under ground; and as soon as they enter'd the City, both Males and Females, young and old, flockt together to see this Lady, holding up their Paws in admiration; at last having brought her into a certain large and spacious Cave, which they intended for her reception, they left her to the custody of the Females, who entertained her with all kindness and respect, and gave her such victuals as they used to eat; but seeing her Constitution neither agreed with the temper of that Climate, nor their Diet, they were resolved to carry her into another Island of a warmer temper; in which were men like Foxes, onely walking in an upright shape, who received their neighbours the Bear-men with great civility and Courtship, very much admiring this beauteous Lady; and having discoursed some while together, agreed at last to make her a Present to the Emperor of their World; to which end, after she had made some short stay in the same place, they brought her cross that Island to a large River, whose stream run smooth and clear, like Chrystal; in which were numerous Boats, much like our Fox-traps; in one whereof she was carried, some of the Bear- and Fox-men waiting on her; and as soon as they had crossed the River, they came into an Island where there were Men which had heads, beaks and feathers, like wild-Geese, onely they went in an upright shape, like the Bear-men and Fox-men: their rumps they carried between their legs, their wings were of the same length with their Bodies, and their tails of an indifferent size, trailing after them like a Ladie's Garment; and after the Bear- and Fox-men had declared their intention and design to their Neighbours, the Geese- or Bird-men, some of them joined to the rest, and attended the Lady through that Island, till they came to another great and large River, where there was a preparation made of many Boats, much like Birds nests, onely of a bigger size; and having crost that River, they arrived into another Island, which was of a pleasant and mild temper, full of Woods and the Inhabitants thereof were Satyrs, who received both the Bear- Fox- and Bird men, with all respect and civility; and after some conferences (for they all understood each others language) some chief of the Satyrs joining to them, accompanied the Lady out of that Island to another River, wherein were many handsome and commodious Barges; and having crost that River, they entered into a large and spacious Kingdom, the men whereof were of a Grass-Green Complexion, who entertained them very kindly, and provided all conveniences for their further voyage: hitherto they had onely crost Rivers, but now they could not avoid the open Seas any longer; wherefore they made their Ships and tacklings ready to sail over into the Island, where the Emperor of the Blazing- world (for so it was call'd) kept his residence. The field moves and changes; our men of Grass-Green complexion change to crimson-skinned Martians and silvery-eyed androids. It is not the same thing over and over again and that is, at least to my mind, a very good thing indeed. And part of that is why writers, even more than readers, should be reading the classics, or at least trying to pick some representative stuff, should have read at least that which includes a solid smattering of works by Isaac Asimov, Lois McMaster Bujold, Edgar Rice Burroughs, Octavia Butler, C.J. Cherryh, Samuel R. Delany, Carol Emshwiller, P.K. Dick, Robert Heinlein, Zenna Henderson, Robert E. Howard, Ursula Le Guin, Fritz Leiber, H.P. Lovecraft, Anne McCaffrey, Andre Norton, Joanna Russ, Cordwainer Smith, Theodore Sturgeon, Jack Vance . . . I need to stop listing names or I'll be here all day, but all of those are voices that have shaped the genre as we know it. And when you hit problematic stuff—because you will, in one form or another, find something tailored to your particular triggers, it's okay to love it if you like.

Can you read everything in the field? Of course not. And you're falling behind in that task even now. But one could, for example, pick up a Nebula Awards collection and get a sampling of that year. Looking at the first one, for example, I see stories by Brian W. Aldiss, J.G. Ballard, Gordon R. Dickson, Harlan Ellison, Larry Niven, James H. Schmitz, and Roger Zelazny.

That's an exclusively male line-up, despite the fact there were women writing at the time, and that leads me to suggest that it's useful not just to read representative works but to get some idea of the context—both the publishing picture at the time various pieces were published and also the larger forces at work in determining what gets remembered and what doesn't. (There's an interesting piece in the most recent *Uncanny Magazine* talking about one of my favorite such books, Joanna Russ's *How to Suppress Women's Writing*, that is well worth reading and very applicable to today.)

If you tell me you are an F&SF writer who can't be bothered to shape their reading around a greater understanding of the field, particularly one that will enhance both one's reading pleasure and writing ability, then I am saddened by what I perceive as a poor choice of priorities on your part.

There are plenty of lists out there. I even helped curate one a few years ago. Sometimes I try to hit at books worth sharing with my You Should Read This posts. And I think it's important to read all over the place, too and not just the same thing over and over again. Mine past centuries for their gems as well as the current bookstore shelves and make it a project idiosyncratic to your interests, your love.

Do we really need a prescribed reader route into learning to love F&SF? No. What we should focus on is creating as many ways into the genre as possible, looking for the shiny lures currently coaxing new readers into the genre and making lists like that—*If you liked the Hunger Games, here's five titles you'd enjoy. Love Star Wars? Here's some space opera. Think the Avengers were awesome? Check out From the Notebooks of Dr. Brain.*

Life's too short to deny yourself good reading. Try reading something you wouldn't normally, something from at least two decades ago. See what you think. You may find it ends up creating a way into an entirely enjoyable labyrinth, lit by the torches older writers ignited, leading the way inward while managing to expand your horizons all at the same time.

ABOUT THE AUTHOR

Cat Rambo lives and writes in the Pacific Northwest, with occasional peregrinations elsewhere. A World Fantasy Award and Nebula nominee, she has 200+ fiction publications, which have appeared in *Asimov's*, *Tor.com*, and *Clarkesworld*, as well as in audio form and a dozen different languages. She is the current President of the Science Fiction and Fantasy Writers of America. Check her website for links to her fiction and information about her popular online classes.

Editor's Desk:
Hibernation Mode Activated
NEIL CLARKE

Some months knock you around. November was one of those for me. The first week was entirely absorbed by World Fantasy Con in Saratoga Springs. Under normal conditions, this would have been relaxing, but I had just come off preparing the November issue and had to pack books for my table in the dealer's room. With the van riding nearly on the ground, Sean and I drove up the night before in hopes of getting a jump on setting-up. That weekend simply reinforced how much I want the old bookstore inventory out of my house and my life. Eight years later, I'm still dragging those boxes around. It's time to find a book dealer and sell the whole thing off.

Despite that, my time outside the dealer's room was enjoyable. Conversations often drifted towards the industry stuff I've talked about in recent editorials and on Facebook. How do we shift the discussion of short fiction magazines from the goals of just merely surviving to growing into a thriving market? Yes, as the magazine editor, I have a vested interest in that path to financial success, but a good chunk of the buzz in my head was been triggered by the introduction I plan to write for *The Best Science Fiction of the Year*. I've been asked to include a state-of-the-market report in my introduction and plan to take the from-ten-thousand-feet view rather than perform a market-by-market analysis. Suffice it to say, no one has the answers, but there's no shortage of ideas. I'm still trying to digest it all.

It would have been nice to have had more time to focus on those concepts, but the submission deadline for *BSFotY* was just a few days later, and naturally, people dropped truckloads of short stories in my inbox in the days leading up to it. My schedule dictated that I dive head-first into the waves and honestly, it almost did me in. I surfaced exhausted, but with Sean's help I made it back to the shores of sanity with my final list intact. After tracking down all the email addresses I needed, I sent the authors their contracts just before I headed off for Philcon.

Philcon was more like a vacation. I wasn't a dealer, didn't make plans outside my list of panels, and just had some fun chatting with people. I knew the month had taken its toll on me when I found myself leaving parties early on Friday night. Normally, I'm a night owl. My body, however, was giving me the warning signs my cardiologists have told me to watch for and listen to. I needed sleep and made sure I got it. In the end, the weekend was a nice balance of relaxing and socializing with fellow SF fans, something I don't get to do often enough. I ended the weekend by having an extremely interesting conversation with Michael Swanwick about writing short fiction. That will also provide me food for thought for some time to come.

The weekend left me refreshed enough to tie up the loose ends on *BSFotY* and the December issues of *Clarkesworld* and *Forever*. Oh, did I mention that I've also accepted the post as interim editor of the SFWA *Bulletin* and signed contracts for two more anthologies? Yeah, I'm a glutton for punishment, but pushing my limits seems necessary if I want to reach the point where I can quit the day job. (Yes, a day job on top of all that.)

So, with the December issues put to bed, I'm going to crash for a little while. I hope you enjoy them.

Happy holidays!

ABOUT THE AUTHOR

Neil Clarke is the editor of *Clarkesworld Magazine, Forever Magazine,* and *Upgraded;* owner of Wyrm Publishing; and a three-time Hugo Award Nominee for Best Editor (short form). The innagural edition of his Year's Best Science Fiction anthology series will be launched by Night Shade Books in 2016. He currently lives in NJ with his wife and two children.

Cover Art:
Kokabiel, Angel of the Stars
PETER MOHRBACHER

Peter Mohrbacher is an independent illustrator and concept artist living in the Chicago area.

WEBSITE

www.vandalhigh.com

www.ingramcontent.com/pod-product-compliance
Lightning Source LLC
Chambersburg PA
CBHW021056130626
46552CB00005B/2134